PHYLLIS MALLETT

MARRIED TO MEDICINE

Complete and Unabridged

LINFORD
Leicester

First published in Great Britain in 1968

First Linford Edition
published 2018

A catalogue record for this book is available
from the British Library.

ISBN 978–1–4448–3581–6

Published by
F. A. Thorpe (Publishing)
Anstey, Leicestershire

Set by Words & Graphics Ltd.
Anstey, Leicestershire
Printed and bound in Great Britain by
T. J. International Ltd., Padstow, Cornwall

This book is printed on acid-free paper

1

'I'll get it, Mother,' Linda Shelton called as the doorbell rang. She threw down the book she was reading and got to her feet. Somewhere in the house the monotonous drone of the cleaner signified that her mother was busy.

They were expecting another house guest. A new doctor was due to arrive at St. Margaret's Hospital, and he had booked to live at Shelton House, where several of his potential colleagues were staying. Linda, herself a doctor at the hospital, was accustomed to her mother's guest house being filled with her colleagues.

She opened the door and stared at the stranger waiting outside. He was tall and his eyes were narrowed against the glare of the sun striking against the white exterior of the house.

'Good morning,' he said stiffly. 'I'm

Dr. Crossley. I believe you're expecting me.'

'Good morning, Doctor,' Linda replied. 'Please come in. Have you just arrived in Redford?'

'It looks like it,' he replied, smiling thinly as he bent to pick up two large cases.

'I wondered if you had stopped off at the hospital before coming here,' Linda said quickly, holding the door wide.

'I'm not that keen on getting started,' he told her, entering the hall.

Linda closed the door and passed him to lead the way to his room. 'Everything is ready for you,' she said, as she started up the stairs. 'When are you reporting at the hospital?'

'I'm not due there until tomorrow,' he said heavily. 'This is a nice place you've got here.' There was animation in his voice for the first time and Linda half-turned to throw a glance at him.

She saw that his face was expressionless, and he looked older than he really was. She knew by the grapevine at the hospital that he was thirty-one, and he was a stickler for work and had no time for women. That much the nurses had learned before his arrival, and Linda smiled wryly to herself when she thought of the discussions that would go on at the hospital when Dr. Crossley started working there.

He was all that they said, she thought grimly. There seemed to be no humour in him. He was a dedicated man, and it seemed that the nurses and other female staff would have to make do with their old friends. Dr. Crossley didn't seem to be a man who would flirt with a pretty nurse.

Mrs. Shelton appeared on the top landing, and she switched off the cleaner when she saw Linda followed by the new guest.

When they reached the top of the stairs, Dr. Crossley set down his cases. Linda introduced him to her mother and he held out his hand.

'I'm pleased to meet you, Dr. Crossley,' Mrs. Shelton said. Her blue eyes were bright as they appraised him. 'I'm sure you'll be quite comfortable here. I've been running this guest house for twenty years, ever since my husband died. He was a doctor, and my daughter Linda takes after him. She's a doctor at St. Margaret's.'

'Are you really?' There was surprise in his voice and he stared at Linda.

'Yes,' she replied, smiling. 'Perhaps I don't look the part, dressed like this, but this is my day off and I like to feel comfortable around the house.'

'Of course — and you have other members of the staff staying here.' He nodded. 'I'm sure I shall be quite comfortable. My needs are simple and you won't find me any trouble.'

'We have a cheerful crowd here,' Mrs. Shelton said. At fifty-three she still looked youthful. She was tall and slender, vivacious, with blonde hair that showed no signs of age. 'Come along and I'll show you into your room. I have no petty restrictions. People come and go as they please. I want you to treat the place as your own home and if there's anything at any time that I can do for you, then please don't hesitate to let me know.'

'Thank you,' he said gravely. He bent to take up his cases, then followed Mrs. Shelton along the landing.

Linda stood listening to her mother chatting gaily as she led the new guest to his room, and when they had gone inside she went slowly down the stairs, back to her book.

So that was Dr. Martin Crossley. Well, the grapevine hadn't exaggerated his manner. They had said he was almost frosty, a doctor in love with his work. It wouldn't affect her, she thought as she sat down and took up her book. She had no interest in men, so they should get along fairly well.

Mrs. Shelton came down the stairs a few minutes later and paused in the doorway of the big sitting-room. 'Aren't you going out today, Linda?'

'I don't think so, Mother. I have some washing to do, and I want to finish this book.'

'Shall we go out after tea?'

'If you like. We could go for a drive.'

'I'll see how I feel later,' Mrs. Shelton promised. 'I do feel tired towards the end of the day.'

'That's because you're doing too much.' Linda put down her book and got to her feet. Crossing to her mother's side, she placed a hand upon her shoulder. 'Why don't you let Lucy's sister come in and help with the heavy work? You know she'd be glad to do so, and Lucy says she has several children and no husband to help her.'

'I'll think it over, dear,' her mother promised. 'Would you like a cup of coffee?'

'I'll make it,' Linda replied with a smile. 'What do you make of Dr. Crossley?'

'I think he'll settle in here very well. He seems to be a quiet type, and he wants to keep himself to himself. I don't like the noisy ones, but thank heavens the majority of the medical staff are responsible people.'

'They have to be, or they wouldn't be in the job,' Linda retorted.

They walked into the kitchen, and Linda made some coffee.

'I'll take up a cup to Dr. Crossley,' her mother said. 'He doesn't want anything else until tea-time. He's going out shortly and won't be back until later.'

'I'll take the coffee up to him,' Linda said firmly. 'You do far too much running around. Sit down now and rest a bit.'

She picked up the cup of coffee and left the kitchen, ascending the stairs to the new boarder's room. Tapping at the door, she waited for his reply. She could hear him moving around inside, and after a few moments the door opened and he peered out at her.

'Hello,' he said, sounding quite friendly. 'Is that for me? Thank you.' He opened the door wide and stepped aside for her to enter, taking the cup and saucer as she passed him. 'So you're at St. Margaret's, too, eh? I was surprised when your mother sprang it on me. I thought you helped in the house here.'

'One can't go by appearances,' Linda answered with a smile.

'How many of your colleagues live here?' he asked, sitting down.

'Six. Most of the unmarried ones. They're all easy to get along with.'

'H'm, I've heard that sort of thing before.' There was a short silence and then he laughed, and the sound contained loneliness and perhaps a little wistfulness. 'Do I sound like a grouch?'

'Not at all,' Linda replied readily. 'We're not all the same, are we? Some people like a lot of noise and others are quiet. Some like a good time and the bright lights and others prefer a good book.'

'That's true. It wouldn't do for all of us to be the same. I'm a quiet one myself. I'm always studying something or other. It was a habit that didn't die when I qualified. Since I finished studying medicine to qualify I've learnt to speak French and now I'm learning German.'

'That's interesting.' Linda stared at him with new interest in her eyes. 'I'm a stick-in-the-mud myself. I had enough of studying when it was necessary.'

He smiled then, and as he did so the seriousness fled from his features. His eyes glinted and he seemed a totally different person to the one who had rung the doorbell a short time before.

'Have you been in this part of the country before?' Linda went on, leaning against the door.

'No, but I don't mind being off the beaten track. Norfolk is rather isolated, isn't it?'

'I prefer that. I spent some time in Leonard's in London and I didn't like it at all. The pace was too fast and life seemed so very much more hectic than here.'

'I'm looking forward to a bit of peace,' he agreed. 'I had thought of going into general practice, but I've

9

shelved the idea for the time being. What about you? Are you happy with what you're doing?'

'Yes. But as I said, I'm a stick-in-the-mud. I'm happy at St. Margaret's and I intend staying there as long as I can.'

He nodded and drank his coffee. 'This is a nice place you have here. It must be cosy for your mother, having nothing but medical people around her.'

'She's been used to it all her life,' Linda said. 'Her father was a doctor, and so was mine. It was inevitable that I should become a doctor and during my student days I used to wonder if it was all worth it, but I wouldn't want to try anything else now. It gets into the blood.'

'I know what you mean.' He smiled. 'Well, I hope I shall settle down in Redford. I liked what I saw of the town when I came in.' He got to his feet and handed the cup and saucer to Linda. 'Thank you for the coffee. Now I must finish unpacking. I want to get along to the hospital and take a look around. You'll have to let me know the timetable of the house. I don't want to get in to meals late or anything like that.'

'The timetables are arranged to suit the boarders,' Linda said with a smile, turning to go. 'There are no limits except common-sense ones.'

'Of course. Thank you for the chat. We must talk again some time.'

Linda nodded and smiled, and left him to finish his settling in. She closed the door and went back to the kitchen, and there was an impression in her mind of Dr. Crossley that was most favourable.

'Linda,' her mother said when she went into the kitchen, 'what on earth have you been doing? Your coffee is quite cold. You shouldn't keep the new boarder from settling in. He has a busy day ahead of him, so he tells me. There'll be plenty of time to get to know him later.'

Linda smiled at her mother's words.

Mrs. Shelton had been trying ever since Linda returned to take up her post at St. Margaret's to get her daughter to take an interest in one of the male staff.

'Let me give you a hand with the housework and then perhaps you'll feel like coming out with me after tea,' Linda said. 'What can I do?'

'Some dusting upstairs,' Mrs. Shelton said. 'There's not much more to be done. Lucy is busy in the kitchen and she won't want any help there.'

Linda nodded as she poured herself a fresh cup of coffee. Lucy Thaine was jealous of the kitchen and never required help, no matter how busy she was. Meals were always served on time and there was never a complaint from any of the boarders. The cooking was always perfect.

'I'll get out the dusters for you, dear.' Mrs. Shelton could never stay in one place long. She had to be busy, no matter the time of day, and as Linda sat down to her coffee her mother hurried out.

Before Linda left the kitchen she heard voices on the stairs and then the sound of the front door. Dr. Crossley had obviously departed. She washed her cup before going to help her mother, and her thoughts were busy on the new boarder as she left the kitchen.

Mrs. Shelton was singing to herself as she put away her cleaning materials. At fifty-three she was well settled in her niche in life. She had no worries and enjoyed every minute of running her guest house. Her life was uncomplicated, except for one cloud upon the horizon — Robert Pearce.

She was thinking of him now. He was a doctor at St. Margaret's and had lived in the house for several years. Lately he had been paying too much attention to Mavis Shelton, and although she liked him well enough there was no thought of a second marriage in her mind, and the indications were that Robert was getting ideas. At forty-five, he was younger than she, and although he was presentable enough she was not the kind of woman to marry twice.

She was startled by Linda's silent approach at her back and turned around with a gasp as Linda spoke to her.

'My dear, you gave me quite a fright! What did you say?'

'I was asking for the dusters,' Linda said, smiling. 'Was that Dr. Crossley who just went out?'

'Yes, dear. He said he'd be back about four-thirty. He's a nice man — I know it instinctively. I'm sure he'll get along quite well with everyone. I like him already and he hasn't been in the house an hour. I never pick the wrong people, do I?'

'You don't, Mother,' Linda agreed seriously, but her eyes were twinkling. 'Pass me those dusters and I'll get to work. You go and sit down and read that magazine I bought yesterday. You should get off your feet more than once a day, if only for a few moments at a time.'

'You're the doctor,' her mother retorted. 'I shall take you at your word.'

Linda smiled as she took the dusters

and went up the stairs. She liked the routine of her life. The work at the hospital was demanding but rewarding, and her leisure time was spent in the house, where she always found something to occupy her. When all the boarders were together in the house, which was seldom, they had discussions that could not otherwise take place, and in the winter, when the sitting-room was cosy with the big fire in the grate, and the evenings were long, there was much to be said for staying in.

She worked vigorously for some time, lost in her thoughts as she went around the various rooms, and it was with some surprise that she heard the sound of a car outside and realised that some of the boarders were coming in to lunch. She went to the window, and peering down at the street saw Robert and Philip Norris alighting from Robert's car. They went into the house and Linda collected her dusters and went down.

Lucy was serving up lunch when

Linda entered the dining-room. Robert and Philip were already seated at the table.

Robert, at forty-five, was tall and heavily built, running almost to fat, and his brown eyes had a piercing quality that always made Linda feel uncomfortable. He was like an uncle to her, but she was aware of his feelings for her mother, and it was a little amusing for her to watch his advances and her mother's accomplished ways of avoiding them.

Philip was thirty-seven and had been married, but his wife had died in a car accident. He was a lonely man who made attempts from time to time at cheerfulness, but he was beginning to drink heavily, and Linda felt sorry for him.

'Hello, Linda,' Robert Pearce greeted loudly. He seemed to be a little too forceful in everything he did. A confirmed bachelor, he was a good doctor and was popular with the nurses at the hospital. 'How are you enjoying

16

your day of rest? Has Mavis got you helping with the housework?'

'I enjoy doing it, Robert,' she replied. 'It makes a change from the rest of the week.'

'I've had a busy morning,' Norris remarked. 'There was a five-car pile-up on the Bexted road this morning. Eight people brought in for treatment, three of them seriously injured. Two people were killed in the smash.' He sighed, and his grave face took on deeper lines as he thought of his dead wife.

'Is Gerald coming in to lunch?' Mrs. Shelton demanded, popping her head around the door. She helped Lucy serve the meals, and that was the only concession the housekeeper-cook permitted.

'Yes. You'll be hearing that motorcycle of his any moment now,' Robert said.

'He was waiting to pick up Stella,' Norris added. 'She was busy when I last saw her. But Colin isn't coming in to lunch today.'

'I know,' Mavis Shelton retorted, and she went back to the kitchen.

Linda moved to the window, from where she could see the street, and shortly she heard a motorcycle, then saw it coming towards the house. Both riders were wearing white crash helmets and she smiled and waved as she was spotted.

Gerald Olley parked the machine while Stella Ingram waited on the kerb for him. Olley was a surgeon and was in his late forties. No one knew why he persisted in riding an ancient motorcycle instead of buying a car, which he could well afford. He had been married, but was divorced, and seemed to have no interest in women.

Stella Ingram was only twenty-eight, and she was a gynaecologist. Linda liked the girl, but their friendship did not extend outside the house because Stella, unmarried, had only one interest — and that was going out with men.

As the pair came into the house Linda turned away from the window.

She was suddenly thinking of the near future, when Dr. Crossley would be meeting his fellow guests, and she knew exactly how Stella would behave. The strange thing was, she did not like the thought of it. Stella had boasted that she would soon bring the newcomer out of his shell, and Stella could do that if it was humanly possible. But the matter was suddenly distasteful to Linda . . .

There was comparative silence at the long table as the meal was eaten, and Linda felt awkward over her thoughts. After the meal there was no hurry by the others to leave the table, and Linda listened to the conversation. Stella wanted to know about the new boarder.

'I've been hearing a lot more about him this morning,' she said. 'Has he arrived, Linda?'

'Yes, he came,' Linda replied in even tones, 'but that reputation which preceded him doesn't seem to fit.' She was wondering why she attempted to defend him. It didn't matter to her what people thought — or did it? She took a deep breath as she lapsed into silence.

'Oh, come on!' Stella said quickly. 'What's he like?'

'Tall and dark,' Linda said with a smile.

'But not handsome?' Stella demanded impatiently.

'Does that make any difference to you?' Philip Norris asked seriously.

'Of course not, Philip.' Nothing could put Stella off. 'But attractiveness helps, or don't you know?'

'My days of dabbling in that rat race they call love and living are over,' Norris replied. 'I always try to find something better to do.'

'But you can't be serious,' Robert Pearce said quickly. 'You're making a big mistake by hiding yourself from the world. There's probably a very nice young woman somewhere out there, and she's just aching for you to come along. You're depriving some girl of her soul-mate.'

'Nonsense!' Gerald Olley snapped,

getting to his feet. 'Philip takes after me. I think that a man, or woman, has only one chance of finding the perfect mate. If you make a mistake you're branded for the rest of your life.'

'It doesn't have to be a mistake,' Norris said thinly. 'I didn't make a mistake. My wife was taken from me. But it's true that nothing is the same again after a deep experience. I wouldn't waste my time trying to find someone to come half up to Sandra.'

'And that's your big mistake, old boy,' Robert Pearce said in his ringing tones. 'You must forget the past. We know it was a terrible blow to you, but you can't go through life like that, you know. You're missing everything. You have to have an inner strength to be able to forget what's happened, but it can be done. Try to put the past into the background and you'll live that much easier.'

'It's easier said than done,' Norris replied, getting to his feet. 'Hadn't we better start back?'

One by one the men drifted away, until only Linda and Stella were at the table.

'Don't they run on so?' Stella demanded. She was tall and attractive, and Linda could never understand why the girl had not married. There were always at least half a dozen men running around Stella, but none of them seemed to get anywhere with her. She went out with a different man each evening, and yet she maintained an aloofness that puzzled Linda.

'And they can sit and say that women talk nonsense most of the time,' Linda declared. 'Men are conceited, aren't they?'

'I don't know what makes them tick,' the other rejoined. 'But I'm always ready to try and find out.' She laughed, getting to her feet. 'I must go, too, or Gerald won't wait for me, and I hate catching a bus. Are you having a nice day off, Linda?'

'You wouldn't think so, in my place,' Linda said cheerfully, 'but it suits me.'

'What's Martin Crossley really like?' Stella paused in the doorway. 'Don't try and keep him to yourself. If I like him I shall take him under my wing.'

'He'll probably find that a bit crowded,' Linda told her, and they both laughed.

'Don't do too much,' Stella retorted, and left.

After helping her mother with the dishes, Linda washed her hair then settled down in her bedroom to read her book. Shortly after four o'clock she joined her mother in the sitting-room.

'Have you thought again about giving up the guest house?' Linda asked. 'Perhaps you could take a cottage out by the Broads, if you prefer the loneliness, although I think it would be a mistake for you to move out of town.'

'I can't make up my mind,' Mrs. Shelton said. 'And what would happen to our boarders if I sold out? Where would they go? We seem to be one big happy family.'

'Not so happy sometimes,' Linda

remarked. 'But I wouldn't suggest a change if you didn't feel so low at times. This house has some bad memories for you.'

'I wouldn't feel happy if I left it,' her mother said softly. 'Your father lived here with us, and he died here. I can't bear to think of strangers occupying the rooms he knew and loved.'

Linda smiled indulgently as she shook her head. This was the way most conversations with her mother went. There was a little bit of the realist in Mavis Shelton, but not enough to dominate the sensitive, sentimental part of her.

'Mother, I think you should go away on a holiday somewhere. Haven't you got an aunt in Scotland? Why don't you write to her and invite yourself up there for a few weeks?'

'But, my dear, what about the house?'

'What about it?' Linda was amused by her mother's horrified air. 'I think we could make satisfactory arrangements about the running of the house. Lucy's sister will welcome the chance of earning some extra money. Now don't tell me you can't afford it.'

'We're fortunate in that your father left us well provided for,' Mavis Shelton said softly. 'But I wouldn't dream of going off and leaving you to cope in your off-duty time.'

'Mother, you know better than that! This place very nearly runs itself, with Lucy in charge.'

'I've got a better idea.' Mrs. Shelton was suddenly enthusiastic. 'Why don't we both go away when you get your holiday? You can take a fortnight in June or July, and we'd have a wonderful time.'

Linda stared at her mother, amazed. Mavis Shelton smiled. She held up a hand before Linda could speak.

'I know, my dear,' she said. 'But I've been neglecting you in the past. We've never been away together, have we? I think you're quite right when you say Lucy can handle everything. If you'd care to make arrangements to take your holiday in June or July, then I'll write

Aunt Harriet and ask her if we can spend two weeks with her.'

'All right,' Linda agreed. 'We'll do it. Go and tell Lucy now so she can start making arrangements, then you won't be able to back out.'

'I like that!' Mrs. Shelton exclaimed. 'You know very well that I never go back on my word once it's been given.' But she got up from the sofa and went out to the kitchen.

Linda followed as far as the door and listened to the animated conversation that took place between her mother and Lucy.

'Eavesdropping?' a voice said at her back, and Linda turned quickly to see Martin Crossley standing on the bottom stair, smiling at her.

'Yes,' she replied with a smile, 'but with good reason. Come into the sitting-room and I'll tell you all about it.' She led the way across the hall into the room. 'I wouldn't want you to get the wrong impression of me,' she said, turning to face him, and told him of her plan to get her mother on holiday. 'She won't budge from the house otherwise,' she ended, 'and I had to make sure she was telling Lucy to make arrangements. Once she's given her word she'll keep it, but it was getting her to make the decision that was so difficult. Now, what kind of a day have you had? Did you get around to the hospital?'

'Oh, yes! I went there first. I met Roland Marlow, and I think he's a great man. I knew of his reputation before I arrived. I shall enjoy working with him. He took me round the various departments, and I met some of your boarders. They seem a nice lot. I think I shall be happy here.'

'Good. That's the main thing. Getting suitable digs is a problem. Mother will treat you as a son if you give her the chance. Have you any family, by the way?'

'Not now.' He spoke in even tones, and his handsome face was expressionless, but Linda felt that he was forcing control upon himself as he spoke. 'My father died before I was born, and my mother died when I arrived. I had an elder brother, but he was killed in a car crash when I was seven.'

'I am sorry.' Linda said gently. 'Poor Philip Norris, who's in charge of Outpatients and lives here, lost his wife in a car accident. Did you meet him at the hospital?'

'Is he tall and thin, very dark, with long bony fingers?'

'Yes.'

'Then I met him. We visited Casualty on the rounds.'

'Did you arrange your day off?' Linda asked.

'As a matter of fact, Marlow mentioned it to me. I'm having Friday.'

'The same day as me!' Linda stared at him. His face was expressionless.

'Yes,' he said, and there was a shadow of a smile. 'That's a coincidence. But I suppose it was because I arrived on a Friday. It wouldn't do for me to start on Monday and get the next day off, would it? Anyway, it doesn't matter to me what day I get off. If anyone wants to change at any time, then you can pass the word around that I'll be glad to co-operate.'

'That's good of you. Sometimes it happens that someone wants to change for one week, and it's the dickens of a job to find someone agreeable to take over.'

Mrs. Shelton came back, beaming, filled with new fire at the thought of the coming holiday. For years she had refused to take even a few days' holiday, but now the decision had been made, the set date couldn't come quickly enough for her.

'It's all arranged, dear,' she said. 'Lucy will see her sister, and if you'll try to get the second and third weeks in June I'll let Aunt Harriet know. But supposing Harriet can't put us up?'

'Then we'll just have to make do in a hotel, like hundreds of other people, Mother,' Linda said with a smile.

'Yes, dear, I suppose so.' Mavis Shelton turned to the silent man. 'So glad to see you back, Dr. Crossley. Did you have a nice day?'

'Splendid, thanks. I went to the hospital and met some of my new colleagues, then had a look around the town.'

'May we get on Christian-name terms?' Mrs. Shelton asked. 'Although everyone does tend to call me Mrs. Shelton. Mavis is so old-fashioned, don't you agree?'

'I think it's a nice name,' he retorted. 'But my name is Martin.'

Mrs. Shelton smiled. 'I'll call you Martin, unless you prefer an abbreviated form.'

'No, I've always been called Martin.'

Linda found herself listening to his voice. It had deep tones, and sounded attractive. She jerked herself from her thoughts when she realised that her mother was talking to her, and Martin was watching her closely. She almost blushed as she caught his eye and saw his slow smile.

'I'm sorry, Mother, but I was miles

away,' she apologised.

'Thinking about the holiday,' Martin said with a grin.

'I was saying, dear, that everyone calls you Linda.'

'Of course.' Linda nodded.

'Then I'll call you Linda, if I may,' he said with no trace of awkwardness.

'With that settled, I think it's time for a cup of tea.' Mrs. Shelton moved to the door, pausing to glance at Martin. 'Do sit down and make yourself at home. When are you starting at the hospital?'

'On Monday,' he replied, moving to an easy-chair and seating himself. 'It's quite a walk, too. I suppose there is a bus service?'

'But there's no need to concern yourself about that,' Mavis Shelton said. 'Linda has a car. If you're working the same hours, she'll give you a lift. All the other guests have their own means of transport, or they share, so you can go with Linda.'

'I'm sure I'd be grateful, if Linda

doesn't mind,' he said, glancing at her.

'I shan't mind in the least,' Linda replied.

'Well, that's soon settled.' Mrs. Shelton went out with a satisfied smile on her face, and Linda laughed inwardly at her mother's attempts to throw the new boarder at her daughter.

'What are you going to do with yourself over the week-end?' Linda asked.

'I think I'll spend some time getting used to Redford, finding my way around, and I'll have to do some studying. It will be my last fling, so to speak, before settling down again to the grind of hospital life.'

'Do you like medicine?' she asked.

'Very much. You could say that I'm married to it.'

'That's what they say about me.' Linda didn't know why she ventured that information, and she flushed a little as he looked at her.

'Well, it's an exacting, demanding life,' he replied. 'I think one has to give a great deal more to medicine than if any other form of work were involved. After all, how often have you arrived home at the end of a heavy day, and then had to ring back to check on a patient?'

'I agree with you,' Linda said, 'but I wouldn't change my work, would you?'

'Emphatically not,' he declared.

They sat talking generally until Mrs. Shelton returned with a tea-tray. With her mother joining in the conversation, the talk covered many more subjects, but kept drifting back to medicine, and then it was time for tea. Mrs. Shelton went off to the kitchen to help Lucy, and the first of the guests returned from the hospital.

Colin Lambert came into the sitting-room, and halted in the doorway when he saw Martin. Lambert was nearly twenty-four, and a houseman at St. Margaret's. He smiled easily as he came farther into the room.

'Hello,' he said cheerfully. 'I missed you when Marlow showed you around.

I'm Colin Lambert, one of the lowest forms of life.'

'This is Martin Crossley, Colin,' Linda said, and Martin got to his feet and held out his hand.

'Pleased to meet you,' Colin said. 'You'll be seeing a lot of me at the hospital. Am I the first one home?'

'Gerald and Stella are coming now, by the sound of it,' Linda said, and a pang stabbed through her heart as she thought of Stella Ingram.

'I don't know why Stella risks her neck on that ancient thing Gerald calls a motorcycle,' Colin put in.

He had a high regard for Stella, and Linda felt sorry for him because he was the last man in the world whom Stella would consider worthy of attention. She flirted with him, but he was taking her seriously, and Linda imagined that trouble would shortly erupt between the two of them.

Stella came quickly into the sitting-room, obviously expecting Martin to be there, and she paused for effect, smiling as Martin got to his feet and waited to be introduced. Stella's words were almost the same as Colin's.

'I missed you at the hospital,' she said in provocative tones, and Linda could not help wincing as she listened. 'I'm Stella Ingram, and you must be Martin Crossley.'

They shook hands, and Stella held on to his fingers when he tried to withdraw them from her hand. An awkward silence began to develop, and Linda tried to retrieve the situation as Martin finally succeeded in getting his hand free.

'What sort of a day have you had, Stella?' Linda asked.

'Usual thing.' Stella turned away carelessly and flopped into a chair. 'I sometimes wish I'd specialised in another branch of medicine, or that women would suddenly develop a whole new range of diseases.' She paused, glanced at Martin, then added: 'I don't have anyone to take me out this evening, and I feel like kicking over the traces a bit.'

'I'm doing nothing tonight, Stella,'

Colin said eagerly. 'There's a good film on at the Regent.'

'I'm past watching films,' Stella said tightly, almost angrily, and she glanced expectantly at Martin, who turned away slowly and resumed his seat.

Linda smiled to herself. Stella didn't take long to swing into action, but she would find it tough going, although resistance would only strengthen the girl's determination. She awaited the girl's next sortie, but before Stella could continue, the rest of the guests began to arrive.

2

Tea was a relaxed meal, and Linda watched Martin closely, without appearing to do so. She found that he was at his ease, despite the pointed remarks that Stella kept firing at him.

Philip Norris surprised Linda by taking a great interest in Martin, asking questions and pursuing unusual lines of conversation with the newcomer. Colin Lambert seemed to be sulking over Stella's refusal to accompany him to the cinema. As for the others, they all greeted Martin cordially, but Robert Pearce had eyes only for Mrs. Shelton, and Linda didn't miss the way her mother's friendship with the man was moving.

Philip Norris was the first to excuse himself from the table, and within moments the others started drifting away. Gerald Olley had to go back on duty, and he left soon after, the sound of his motorcycle reverberating through the house.

Stella lingered at the table because Martin sat talking to Linda. Eventually, during a pause in their conversation, Stella said brightly: 'Are you busy this evening, Martin?'

'I'm afraid I shall be,' he replied.

Linda smiled to herself. Poor Stella was going to find it a rough passage to Martin's heart, but the girl was a compulsive flirt. She just had to try and ensnare every new man she came across, and Martin was no exception. In fact, Stella always took reticence on the part of a male as a challenge.

'Is it anything that I can share in?' Stella went on.

'I don't think so.' Martin was sounding harassed. 'Linda very kindly offered to take me out this evening and show me around.'

He looked at Linda as he spoke and she plainly saw the appeal in his eyes, an almost animal emotion that must surely greet a rescuer approaching some trapped dog. She could hardly prevent a gasp of surprise at his words, but said quickly: 'Mother and I are going out this evening and I thought it only polite to ask Martin along.'

'I see!' Stella got to her feet, clearly aware that she had lost a battle, and there was surprise on her face because this was the first time that she could remember when Linda had asked a man to go out with her. 'Well, some other time,' she continued, making an effort to depart gracefully.

When they were alone Martin turned to Linda and there was a troubled look on his face. 'I'm sorry I dragged you in like that,' he apologised, 'but I had been warned at the hospital to look out for Stella, and I have no wish to get caught up in any affair with her. I thought she might slacken off her ardour a bit if she imagined you had got in first with me. Don't take me wrongly, will you? I didn't want to hurt her feelings by flatly refusing her company.'

'I'm glad you put it as you did,'

Linda replied slowly. 'Stella is a bit much sometimes. She can't help it, you know. But you're welcome to come out with Mother and me this evening if you'd like.'

'I wouldn't dream of intruding,' he replied quickly. 'It was good of you not to give me away, and I'm sure I won't impose upon you.'

'I would have asked you had I thought you might be interested in a drive, but I was afraid that you'd think I was forward, so I wouldn't broach it.'

'You're not at all like Stella, are you?' He laughed, then he sighed. 'But perhaps I'd better take you up on an invitation, just in case Stella plays it smart and watches for me to accompany you.'

'All right, so I'll make it a formal invitation.' Linda smiled as she spoke, but she was aware that her heart was beating fast. 'Martin, would you like to come for a drive with Mother and me this evening?'

'I should enjoy it,' he replied in

mock-serious tones. 'What time will you be leaving?'

'Will seven be too soon for you?'

'Not at all, and I promise not to keep you waiting.' He grinned, and there was none of the tension now in his face.

'I wouldn't do this for just anyone,' Linda told him lightly, 'but as this is your first day here, and I wouldn't want to see you caught up in Stella's toils, I'll make an exception.'

'I promise that I shan't ever bother you again,' he retorted, and although the grin was still on his lips there was a shadow in his eyes.

'Well, I'd better go find Mother and tell her,' Linda said quickly. 'I wouldn't put it past Stella to make enquiries in that direction.'

He nodded, getting to his feet, and they left the room together. Linda went into the kitchen to find her mother talking to Lucy, and she suddenly felt shy and tongue-tied as they broke off their conversation to listen to her.

'Mother, I hope you don't mind, but

I've asked Martin to take a drive with us this evening.'

'You have, dear?' There was a sudden sparkle in Mrs. Shelton's eyes and she threw a quick glance at the house-keeper. 'Well, that's a bit of luck, isn't it?'

'What do you mean?' Linda was suddenly very still.

'I was about to come and tell you that I've got a headache coming on. I didn't want to disappoint you by not going out, because it is your day off, but if Martin is going with you then I can go and lie down with an easy mind.'

'You mean you're not coming this evening?' Linda demanded.

'It wouldn't be any fun for me, not with a splitting headache, would it, dear?'

'Mother, you wouldn't do this to me, would you?' Linda implored. 'You haven't got a headache and you know it. You're an opportunist, that's what you are. I know when you've got a headache, so don't try to fool me.'

'I assure you that I have, and it's really bad, getting worse every moment.' Mrs. Shelton was adamant. 'But I'm sure you'll have a nice time with Martin. He seems a very fine man. He's a stranger here and it's up to you to make him feel at home. Now off you go and get ready. I'll go and lie down and rest.'

Linda took a long breath, shaking her head as she stared at her mother, but deep inside she was trying to control a feeling of relief that threatened to rise up and swamp her. She sighed heavily, conscious now that she was acting her horror, that it had fled before the onset of other, deeper emotions.

'All right,' she said heavily, trying not to overdo it, 'if you're going to let me down like this, then you needn't bother to write Aunt Harriet about the holiday. I shan't go.'

'You are a good girl,' Mrs. Shelton said with a smile. 'I agreed to go in a rash moment and I've been regretting the decision ever since. Now you've said you don't want to go either I can forget it with an easy mind.'

'Mother!' Linda exclaimed, but there was a smile on her lips. 'All right, I'm going this evening, but I'll make you pay for this.'

'Just be pleasant with Martin and make him feel at home. I've been telling you for years to get out and about with a nice young man. It seems to me that Martin coming here has a touch of Providence about it. What time are you going?'

'Seven.'

'All right. I'm going up to rest now, and if my head is better by seven then I'll come with you. Will that suit you?'

'Mother, you know you won't show your face out of your room until I've gone,' Linda said. 'I can see your little plan and I don't like it. You're as bad as Stella, but I'm going to hold you to that holiday in Scotland.'

'I'll go with you,' Mrs. Shelton said with surprising meekness, 'but by the time June gets here you may not want to go.'

'And what do you mean by that?' Linda demanded.

'I'm sure I don't know, dear,' her mother replied with a smile. 'I'm such a rambler that I don't understand the half of what I say.'

Linda shook her head and left the kitchen, followed by the sound of Lucy's laughter, and she knew that her mother had scored a triumph, but she was not put out by it. Thinking of Martin Crossley, she nodded to herself. There was something about him that attracted her though she couldn't put her finger on it.

On the stairs to her room she paused and a hand went to her throat as a thought struck her. Perhaps Martin wouldn't want to go out with her when he learned that her mother wasn't going along? She wondered why she should feel upset about it. Martin was a stranger; a good-looking stranger, but she had met good-looking men before. Was she feeling pity for him? She shook her head slowly as she tried to analyse her feelings and failed. There seemed to be a sense of anticipation building up inside her and that was most peculiar. She went on to her room and began to prepare for the evening, and as the minutes passed and the appointed hour drew near she began to feel nervous.

At seven she left her room and went slowly down the stairs. There were voices in the sitting-room, and as she paused by the door, it suddenly opened and Martin appeared.

He smiled at her, and Linda stepped back hurriedly as she heard Stella's voice. Martin followed her, closing the door quickly.

'Phew, I had to get away from Stella,' he said. 'Are you ready?' He glanced at his watch.

'I am, but I'm afraid Mother is not,' Linda said, aware that her tones were stiff and formal. 'She's got a headache and has gone to rest.'

'Oh.' He stared at her for a moment, then nodded slowly. 'Well, that's all right. So we'll call it off. I have plenty of other things to do.'

'But I'm still going,' Linda went on. 'What I mean is, there's no need to upset the arrangements just because Mother isn't coming. I'm going for a drive and you're welcome to come along.'

'Thanks for the offer. It's kind of you to give up an evening for me. You don't want to go driving on your own?'

'Not really,' she replied, aware that her heart was beating rapidly. 'So you have a choice to make,' she said, with a small laugh. 'Which is the lesser of the two evils?'

He smiled broadly. 'You've got a nice way of putting it,' he remarked. 'I'll go with you, if I may. But perhaps we'd better not let Stella see us leave alone or she may come out to keep us company.'

'The car is in the garage at the back of the house. We can go out the back door, so no one will see us. Come along. Stella may be getting impatient in there and once she takes to the warpath nothing short of a scalp will appease her. I just want to see if Mother is all right.'

Linda left Martin waiting near the kitchen and went along to the small room that had been her father's study in the old days. Tapping at the door, she opened it quickly and peered inside, to find her mother seated by the window, knitting furiously.

'Mother,' she said, going into the room and closing the door. 'Some headache that turned out to be. You're the very limit.'

'You run along and enjoy yourself with Martin. It's about time you found someone to go around with.'

'All right.' Linda smiled thinly. 'I'll have to go because Martin is waiting. See you when I get back.'

'Have a nice time, dear,' Mrs. Shelton retorted.

Relief seemed to blossom up inside Linda as she led Martin out through the kitchen door to the garage. As they got into her car she smiled. Now they were beyond Stella's reach for the evening.

She drove smoothly out of the garage and along the wide path to the back street. Martin settled himself in his seat and gazed around as they went through the built-up area.

'You drive well,' he remarked shortly.

'Thank you,' she replied, and now they were alone she was feeling slightly self-conscious, something which hadn't afflicted her since her teens. 'Do you drive?'

'I can, but I don't very often. This is a nice little car though.'

Linda felt more relaxed as they went along and soon was chatting easily to him. They reached the outskirts of the town and began to drive into the surrounding country. The evening was cool, but bright, and the sun was still showing above the trees to the west.

It seemed like a dream, Linda told herself as the evening drew on. Here she was out with a man and enjoying every moment of his company. In her teens she had had enough boy-friends to last her a lifetime, and although some of them had become serious over her, none of them had been able to start a blaze in her heart.

She had taken to studying medicine because of the satisfaction it had given her, and she had relished those long hours of training because there had always been ample excuse to cloister herself away with her books, and friends had been fobbed off by her excuses because they had been so real. But that sort of thing made for a lonely life. Her mother had been telling her so for a good many years, but Linda had heard only with her ears and not with her mind. Now a few short hours in this man's company had brought home the truth.

Darkness came, and still Linda drove on, wanting this trip to last for ever. If only she could go on and on without ever turning back! The thought rose unbidden in her mind, and she was startled by it.

'Would you care to stop somewhere for a drink?' Martin asked suddenly. 'Or don't you believe in drinking and driving?'

'I don't mind one gin and orange,' she replied, 'but there I draw the line.' She paused, and glanced at him. 'You do drink?'

'Yes. I suppose I've got all the known vices, except smoking. You don't smoke?'

'No. I detest the habit.'

'Then we should be very good friends. I hope you'll take up languages. I should like to teach you.'

'You'll be busy then.' Linda laughed, her mind on the road ahead. 'Stella will take you up on it, too, you know. She won't let the grass grow under her feet.'

'She won't take no for an answer,' he replied. 'She's outrageously brazen, isn't she?'

'You'll get used to her. If you don't want anything to do with her and you can manage to make it quite plain, she'll eventually give you up, but only if someone new comes along. I've never met a girl like her before.'

'There's no harm in her,' Martin said

gently. 'I think she's rather a lonely soul. Has she any family?'

'A father living somewhere, but she doesn't get many letters. I think you're right — Stella must be a very lonely person.' Linda paused, then went on: 'You should get along with the rest of the boarders, though. But if you take them as a cross section of people in the medical profession it points to the fact that a great many of our doctors are unmarried.'

'It's a profession that one can easily marry,' he said. 'You seem to have landed yourself in the same situation, and I'm thirty-one and unattached. There didn't seem to be time for a normal growing-up period in my life. I don't know if others in the same circumstances found it similar, but I didn't have an adolescence, so it seems.'

'I know what you mean. And once you get working in a hospital time seems to lose all significance. The routine gets hold of you, and you plod on until one day you realise that you're old, and there are younger people on the ladder all trying to push you off and take your place.'

'Are you thinking like that already?' he demanded, smiling. 'You sound as if you're forty-seven instead of twenty-seven.'

'Who told you my age?' she countered quickly.

'Your mother.'

'I see. I shall have to talk severely to her. Can't have her giving away my secrets.' Linda laughed and fell silent. She was enjoying herself immensely, and could tell that he, too, was pleased with the evening's excursion. She was glad she had asked him to come and that her mother had cried off.

They stopped at a little inn for a drink, and when they emerged again into the darkness Linda asked Martin if he would care to drive. He shook his head.

'Some other time, perhaps, when I know the roads. You're doing very well, Linda, so keep going.'

As she drove back to town, she wondered if he would want to go out with her again, and it didn't surprise her to know that she wanted him to.

* * *

The next day being Saturday, Linda had to be at the hospital in the morning as usual, but she was free in the afternoon. The evening, however, would see her back on duty until ten.

The day was warm and sunny, in keeping with her feelings. She had never felt happier, and she hummed to herself as she drove to the hospital.

Linda arrived at the hospital car-park the same time as Stella Ingram and Gerald Olley, and as Linda got out of her car and locked the door Stella came towards her.

'You're a dark horse, Linda, and no mistake,' the girl said. 'What are you up to with Martin Crossley?'

'Stella, I don't know what you're talking about,' Linda replied as they walked together towards the big hospital block. 'You're always talking in riddles, my girl. What's on your mind this time?'

'Your mother didn't go out with you last night!' Stella accused good-naturedly.

'So is it a crime for me to go out alone with a member of the opposite sex?' There was levity in Linda's tones, and she knew Stella was taking it all in good part.

'Have you taken a fancy to him, then? If so, I'll keep off, but if you don't have any designs on him then stay away and leave me a clear field.'

'That's a nice way to put it,' Linda countered.

'That's the way I see it. I don't wear rose-tinted glasses, Linda. Life isn't like that. If you see something you want in this world then you've got to grab it with both hands, and before the other girl gets in. So let me have it straight. Are you getting ideas about Martin?'

'Are you?' Linda demanded.

'Yes, but I don't want to get in the

way of the big romance of your life. Tell me if you're interested and I'll cast my net in other waters, but if you don't have any feelings for him then let me at him!'

'Stella, I do believe you're getting worse as you get older.' Linda didn't know how to avert the girl's direct attack.

'Not getting worse, just getting more serious.' Stella wasn't treating the matter lightly any more. 'Martin Crossley seems just the type of man I've always been looking for.'

'But how can you tell in such a short time? You didn't meet him until yesterday evening.'

'How long does a girl need to find out that the man she's met is the one she wants to spend the rest of her life with?' Stella laughed harshly. 'Life is very short, my little innocent, and it isn't always sweet. Can I take it that you haven't suddenly lost your heart to this handsome stranger? It would be ironic indeed if we both fell for him at the same time, and he with the reputation of not liking women!'

'Stella, I sometimes wonder about your sanity,' Linda said, pushing open a door and stepping aside for the girl to enter the building in front of her.

Stella sighed. 'I didn't think I'd get an answer out of you, Linda. Either you're too naïve to be true or else you're the world's deepest girl.'

'I'll see you later,' Linda told her, hurrying away along the wide corridor, glad that Stella's department was on the other side of the hospital.

But she was worried as she reached her office. If Stella was getting serious about Martin, then her own chances were as good as dead. She took off her coat and put on the white coat she wore around the wards. She was no match against the more experienced Stella and her own efforts at ensnaring Martin would seem like child's play.

But what was she doing thinking about the new boarder in such a manner? She should have been shocked by the knowledge that he could arouse strange emotions inside her, but she was not, and her heart beat faster as she recalled the evening before.

They had spent several hours in one another's company, and she had loved every minute of it. In fact, she could hardly wait to see him again. In a matter of hours, he had become of utmost importance in her life — and as she faced this fact, Linda realised that she was falling in love with the man.

Her first duties in the mornings were to make a round of the wards under her supervision, and she felt less like working this morning than she had ever done before.

A tap at the office door had her swinging around in confusion, and she closed her eyes and tried to compose herself as she called out an invitation to enter. The door opened and Sister Kirtland entered, smiling, her usual cheery, efficient self.

'Good morning, Doctor.'

'Good morning, Sister. Have you got

those reports for me?'

'They're on your desk. I thought I'd come and talk to you about them after your round.'

'Yes. I must get around the wards now.' Linda was aware that her eyes were shining, and her cheeks were flushed. She hoped no one would notice and put the correct diagnosis upon her condition.

'Are you feeling well, Dr. Shelton?' The Sister was keen-eyed, and trained to notice the smallest detail.

'I'm feeling fine,' Linda replied. 'Why do you ask?'

'You have a lot of colour, and your eyes are rather bright. You don't have a fever, do you?'

'I don't think so, and I feel perfectly well.' Linda unbent a little, smiling. 'I expect it's the time of the year. It's a relief to see bright sunny mornings after all that frost and bad weather.'

'If I didn't know you better I'd say you were in love,' Sister Kirtland commented, and Linda smiled.

'Well, you do know me better, so don't go spreading any rumours around the hospital. I may be a little excited this morning because my mother has at last agreed to take a holiday with me this year.'

'Oh, lovely! You've been wanting to get her away for a long time. Where will you go?'

'To Scotland, most probably. She has an aunt living up there, and we used to go there each year when I was a girl. It will be nice to see the old places again.'

'I was beginning to think that your new boarder had something to do with it.'

'My new boarder?' Linda repeated innocently.

'Yes. Everyone here is raving about him, and I've heard that Dr. Ingram has got her eye on him already.'

'Well, you mustn't believe everything they feed into that grapevine,' Linda said firmly.

They left the office and walked along the corridors to the first ward. Then they began a round of the patients, and for a time Linda was able to push all personal thoughts into the back of her mind.

Her round over, Linda returned to her office, checked the memos on her desk, and was just about to leave again when the phone rang. It was Stella.

'Linda, will you drive me home at lunch? Gerald is staying here until six this evening, and I don't feel like catching a bus. You'll be going about twelve, won't you?'

'Yes, if I don't get any interruptions,' Linda replied, glancing at her watch. 'Be in the car-park on time and you can have a lift.'

'See you then,' came the brief reply, and the line went dead.

Linda replaced the receiver and left the office, a sigh rippling from her. She was lost in thought as she went along the corridor, and turning a corner she walked into a big figure coming from the opposite direction. A strong hand grasped her elbow as she staggered from the impact, and then Robert Pearce's ringing tones sounded.

'Linda, you're day-dreaming. I'm big enough to see. What on earth have you got on your mind?'

'I'm sorry, Robert. I didn't hurt you, did I?'

'Not at all. I'm still pretty nifty on my feet, despite my size. But this is a stroke of luck. It was wondering if I could catch you this morning before you left. Are you very busy? I'd like to have a talk with you.'

'I can spare you a few moments,' she replied, looking at her watch.

'Come along to my office, then. I shan't keep you long.' Pearce turned, taking her elbow as they started back along the corridor.

Linda sat down on the chair placed beside the large desk for visitors, and watched Robert's face as he sat down. He was a tall man with a big frame, in his middle forties, and the flesh was beginning to sag on his jawline. His brown eyes were narrowed, calculating, and she began to wonder at his reason for wanting to see her.

'Linda, I want to ask your mother to marry me,' he said tensely. He said no more, apparently waiting to see her reactions to his surprising statement.

Linda blinked, but her expression did not change. For a moment there was silence in the office. Then she took a deep breath. 'Surely you should put the question to Mother before telling me about it,' she said softly.

'I know.' He spoke in his pompous way. 'But I wanted to know if you'd have any objections.'

'But why should I? It's none of my business. Surely you should be more concerned over Mother's objections.'

'I don't think Mavis will refuse me.' He was smiling now. 'But you're her daughter, and as such you're the only rival for her affections. It would change her whole life, of course, and I should want you to be in complete agreement with the marriage. There would have to be some changes. The guest house would have to cease as such. We could go on living there, and you would stay on, of course. But how does the idea strike you?'

'I must say that it's none of my business, and it's up to Mother to make her own decisions. Propose to her by all means, but don't expect her to accept as readily as you may imagine. Mother is a shrewd woman underneath that charm of hers.'

'I haven't offended you by mentioning this, have I?' He got to his feet and came around the desk, standing head and shoulders over her as she arose and faced him.

'I'm not offended, Robert,' she said slowly. 'It just has nothing to do with me, that's all. I wish you had spoken first to Mother.'

'I intend doing that today, when I get the chance,' he replied. 'If she does accept, then I shall become your stepfather.'

Linda smiled politely, but made no reply.

'Perhaps it's something of a shock to you,' he went on. 'I did rather spring it out of the blue. Take some time to think it over, and if you can let me know your reactions before I speak to your mother I should appreciate it.'

'All right, Robert.' Linda glanced at her watch. 'Now I really must be going. I don't want to be late today.'

She turned away, and he hurried around her to open the door. 'See you later,' he said, smiling. 'It was good of you to spare me the time.'

Linda smiled and hurried away, her mind seething with his words. But she was not shocked so much by the knowledge that he was going to propose to her mother as she was by the news that he wanted the house to be turned into a private residence. He wanted to live in the place alone with her mother.

She caught her breath as she imagined the big house empty, and her eyes narrowed when she realised that Martin would have to leave with the others. But her mother would never agree to that, whatever she did about the proposal. The guest house had been her whole life far too long for her to give it up for any reasons less than ill health.

3

The rest of the morning passed in a whirl, and Linda was surprised when she returned to her office to find Stella waiting impatiently there. She glanced at her watch and saw the time was ten past twelve.

'Don't tell me your days are always as busy as this,' Stella said. 'You told me to be waiting in the car-park at twelve. You'll have to specialise, dear girl, and cut down on some of this dashing around.'

'Sorry, Stella, but I got delayed a couple of times. Then Robert side-tracked me for a few moments, and I never seemed to get ahead again.'

'Well, are you ready now?' the girl asked.

'Just give me time to take off this white coat,' Linda replied with a smile.

When she was ready they left the

office and went out to the car-park. As they were getting into the car Stella reached out and clutched at Linda's arm.

'Isn't that Martin over there? Look, just outside the gate. He's at the bus stop. Do you suppose he would like a lift home?'

'We could ask him,' Linda answered, suddenly feeling nervous.

She set the car in motion and drove out of the car-park, halting in the wide gateway, and she gazed at Martin Crossley standing a few yards away at the bus stop.

'I'll call him,' Stella said enthusiastically, and opened the door of the car and sprang out to the pavement.

Linda watched her hurry across to Martin, and he turned quickly to stare at the car as the girl spoke to him. They came back together, and Linda felt her heartbeats quicken as he bent to stare at her.

'Hello,' he said. 'I had no idea you would be leaving at this time or I would have waited for you. I was waiting for a bus to take me home.'

'Get in then, and you'll save the fare,' Linda told him.

Stella and Martin quickly got into the car, and Linda headed homewards.

'Have you been at the hospital this morning?' Stella asked Martin, and he nodded.

'Yes. There was a point I wanted to raise with Roland Marlow.'

'And you came to see him about it?' There was surprise in Stella's voice. 'Aren't you afraid of anything? No one on the staff would approach old Marlow unless it was strictly necessary.'

'Really?' Martin was slightly amused, as Linda saw when she glanced quickly at his profile. 'I found him a very nice person when I spoke to him yesterday.'

'Well, you may be one of the favoured few,' Stella said grudgingly, 'but he's the terror of the nurses and the housemen.' She widened her smile, leaning forward until her face was close to Martin's right ear. 'I'm off duty for the rest of the day, but Linda will be working this evening. Isn't it my turn to have your company for a bit?'

Linda was amazed by the girl's nerve, and she glanced at Martin, wondering how he would get out of it. He was smiling thinly, completely at ease.

'I'm sorry, but I made arrangements just before I left the hospital to see a couple of old friends this evening. Frank Pye and Tom Sutton were both at St. Timothy's when I was there, and we're having a kind of reunion.'

'I see.' Stella was quite unabashed. 'Some other time, then. But it seems to me that Fate is preventing us from getting together.'

They drove home in silence, Linda wondering if Fate would go on preventing Stella from getting together with Martin, and deep in her heart she prayed that it would do so.

As they entered the house, Mrs. Shelton came out of the kitchen, pausing in the doorway. 'Hello,' she greeted them, 'lunch is ready. I'm glad to see you back, Martin. Did Linda give you a lift?'

'Yes.' He glanced at Linda, and Stella, half-way up the stairs, paused and looked down at them, her face showing enquiry. 'I happened to be at the hospital just as she was coming out.'

'And ordinarily she would have been alone,' Stella remarked, continuing on her way. 'I think there's some manoeuvres taking place on the side. Well, well!'

Linda stared after the girl, but made no comment, and she felt her heart racing. Martin was grinning, and Mrs. Shelton laughed.

'When Martin said he was going to town this morning, I mentioned that you would be leaving the hospital about twelve,' she said. 'I thought it would be nice for him to ride home with you, Linda.'

'I was late coming out this morning,' Linda said as Stella disappeared on the landing. 'The buses run every seven minutes. Did you let some of them go by while you waited for me to appear?'

'Certainly not.' There was gentleness in Martin's voice, and his face was grave. 'I arrived there late, and went into the hospital, you remember? I saw two old friends, and spoke to Roland Marlow. When I came out I thought you had gone.'

'Well, you picked him up, didn't you?' Mrs. Shelton said, smiling. 'That's the main thing. Always help one another. I found that always worked in my time.'

'Always worked what?' Linda demanded. She was not displeased with the way the conversation had gone, but she did not show it.

'You run along and prepare for lunch,' Mrs. Shelton said. 'I want to talk to you later about something that's very important.'

'You'd better tell me now if it is important,' Linda said.

'It's not that important, silly.' Her mother smiled benignly. 'Lunch will be served in five minutes.'

Linda hurried to her room to freshen up before lunch, and when she went downstairs Martin was already in the sitting-room. Philip Norris had come in, and he was chatting animatedly to Stella, who was seated in a corner, looking very austere. Martin was reading the newspaper, but he laid it aside when he saw Linda, and smiled engagingly.

'Perhaps you'll let me drive your car one of these odd evenings,' he remarked, and Stella paused in the middle of what she was saying to Philip and stared across the room.

'I said you could drive it whenever you wished,' Linda replied.

'I'm thinking of buying a car,' Martin went on, and his tones were casual. 'If I like the way yours handles, then I'll get one.'

'I'm on duty this evening until ten,' Linda said. 'You could drop me off at the hospital at six, and collect me at ten, unless you're doing something else. In between you can go where you please.'

'That's a good idea,' he replied quickly. 'I do have to go out this evening to meet

Frank and Tom, but I don't want to be in late, and I know what they are. So I can tell them that I have to pick you up at ten.'

Linda smiled. She could see the expression of disbelief on Stella's face, but she didn't care. Even a short drive home from the hospital in Martin's company would be something.

She sat down in a corner and pretended to glance through a magazine, but the print was indistinguishable to her blurred eyes. She tried to control her emotions, and wondered what was happening inside her. Why could this stranger evoke such feelings in her breast? He had immense powers over her, and it was a relief to her that he did not know it.

When they were called into the dining-room, Martin managed to get behind Linda, and Stella found herself walking on ahead with Philip Norris. Martin sat beside Linda at the table, and Mrs. Shelton beamed happily when she came in and saw them together.

They had barely started the meal when Colin Lambert appeared.

'There was a fearful accident at the crossroads in the market place,' the young houseman said, sitting down in the vacant place at Stella's side. 'A lorry collided with a bus. There were three ambulances taking away the injured.'

'They should put lights at that crossing,' Mrs. Shelton said. 'I suppose Robert will be late now. He rang a short time ago to say that he had an emergency on his hands.'

'Probably Mrs. Hayman,' Colin said. 'She was in under observation, and there was something of a mystery about her condition. Twice this morning Robert decided to operate, then called it off.'

The talk followed a similar vein through the meal, and afterwards Colin and Philip went back to the hospital. Stella collected a couple of books and went up to her room, and Linda adjourned to the sitting-room, followed a short time later by Martin.

They chatted for a few minutes, then Mrs. Shelton appeared in the doorway, obviously wanting to speak to her daughter. Linda was sorry when Martin excused himself and left the room. Her mother came across to the sofa and sat down.

'I must say that you're getting very friendly with Martin,' Mrs. Shelton said.

'Thanks largely to your efforts, Mother dear,' Linda retorted lightly.

'Well, he's a nice man, and I could see that he was terribly lonely the moment I set eyes on him. You're looking brighter since he arrived. You two must be good for one another.'

'Never mind that,' Linda said fiercely, although her expression belied her tones. 'What was that important matter you wished to talk over?'

'Oh, that!' Mrs. Shelton smiled. 'I do believe I've forgotten.'

'Mother, you are the limit! It couldn't have been very important if you've forgotten it.'

'No, it's come back to me,' Mrs. Shelton said teasingly. 'I rang Aunt Harriet this morning because I couldn't wait to find out if she could have us in June.'

'And?' Linda prompted, when her mother lapsed into silence.

'We can go up any time we choose this year.'

'Well, that seems to settle it.' Linda spoke firmly. 'We'll take the last two weeks of June. I checked this morning and they are vacant at the moment. It's a bit early for the rest of the staff, so I'll make a note of it this evening. Have you spoken to Lucy about her sister standing in for you?'

'That's all taken care of.' Mrs. Shelton smiled. 'I can be businesslike when I have to. Lucy will tell her sister when we want to leave, and she'll come in. She's a capable woman, by all accounts, so we'll have no need to worry about anything until we come back.'

Linda thought of her talk with Robert Pearce that morning, and wondered how her mother would take the proposal. She studied her mother's face as her thoughts meandered, and she knew she wanted the future to be happy beyond all other considerations. Her mother deserved that.

'Mother, I asked you some time ago when you felt that this place was getting you down to consider selling up and moving into a flat. You've only half replied to my questions about it since. Have you thought about it?'

'No, dear,' Mrs. Shelton replied. 'It would have been a waste of time. You know I wouldn't give up this place for anything in the world.'

'Anything?' Linda prompted.

'Anything!' Mrs. Shelton turned to face her daughter. 'What are you getting at? Is there anything on your mind?'

'What could be on my mind?' Linda demanded.

'I don't know, but there's a strange look in your eye, and I know it quite well. Are you planning something, or just thinking ahead?'

'I'm doing neither,' Linda protested. 'Why should I be doing anything at all? I'm just curious. I wanted to know how much importance you attach to this place.'

'It's my whole life, dear,' her mother replied firmly. 'I'm going to finish up my days here, taking care of the unattached members of St. Margaret's staff. I like the atmosphere they give to the house. I would certainly miss them if they had to leave for any reason.'

'Well, I can't think of any reason that could crop up to take them away from you.' Linda kept her fingers crossed. 'I don't suppose the hospital authorities will build an accommodation block for the staff. They haven't got enough money to build bed space for the patients.'

'What are you going to do this afternoon?' Mrs. Shelton asked.

'Nothing at all. I'm going to laze around until five, then have tea and get ready for duty. I shall report to the hospital at six, and stay there until ten.'

'I'm going out this afternoon,' Mrs. Shelton said. 'I want to do some shopping. I thought you might like to come, but if you're feeling lazy, then don't stir.'

'Do you really want me to come?' Linda asked.

'No, it's all right. Robert said he would walk with me, but he hasn't come home yet. He must have been caught up in the flood of patients from that accident Colin mentioned.'

'I'll get ready, if you like,' Linda offered.

'No, my dear, you have a rest. I'm all ready to go, and I want to leave immediately.'

Linda nodded, and her mother got to her feet and left the room.

'See you when I get back, dear,' she called, and paused in the doorway. 'Is there anything you want while I'm out?'

'No, thank you.' Linda settled herself down and closed her eyes. She dozed almost against her will, and fell asleep. A sound brought her sharply to her senses, and she opened her eyes and sat up quickly, glancing around the room.

Martin sat in a chair by the window, watching a scene outside, but it wasn't he who had awakened her. Robert had come in, his fleshy face showing strain. Linda glanced at her watch, and saw the time was nearly four. She swung her legs to the floor and blinked as she tried to collect her sleep-scattered wits.

'I'm sorry, did I wake you?' Robert asked, his dark eyes studying her.

'That's all right,' Linda conceded. 'I'm glad you did. I meant to do some work this afternoon.'

'I would have called you,' Martin told her with a smile, 'but I didn't know how long you wanted to rest, and you looked far too comfortable to be disturbed.'

'I've had the most dreadful time,' Robert said. 'I suppose you heard about the accident at lunch-time? I was just finishing off an emergency when the first of the casualties were brought in. I worked nonstop for three hours. It would have to happen on a Saturday, when there's only a skeleton staff on duty.'

'If you'd thought to ring here I would have come along to help,' Martin said.

'Never thought about it, old boy. The pressure was too great at that end, anyway. Never mind, it's all over with now.'

'Has Mother returned yet?' Linda asked.

'I haven't seen her,' Martin replied. 'It's been peaceful in here, except for your snoring.'

'Go on with you, I wasn't snoring.' Linda stared at him, and saw that he was smiling. He wasn't at all stiff and distant when one got to know him, she thought. He was totally different now to the man who had been on the doorstep when she answered the bell yesterday.

'No, it was someone sawing wood out at the back,' he retorted, and Linda picked up a small cushion and tossed it at him.

Robert tut-tutted and strode out of the room, and Linda got to her feet.

She felt light-hearted as she moved to the door. In the doorway she paused and turned to look at Martin, and found him gazing after her. He was smiling broadly.

'I shall be ready to leave here at a quarter to six,' she said. 'I mustn't be late this evening if they've had an influx of injured. It looks like being a busy evening.'

'It will help to make the time go faster,' he retorted. 'I'll be ready.'

Linda went up to her room and began to prepare for evening duty. Her thoughts were deep as she stared at her reflection in the dressing-table mirror while doing her hair. Was Martin attracted to her? A week ago she wouldn't have thought it possible that she could be sitting here and so calmly pondering over a man's feelings for her. But the really surprising thing was that she hoped he had been attracted, that he did want to know her better and see something of her during their off-duty hours.

It had been bound to happen, she had been told many times by friends. One day there would be a man who mattered! She had never believed it, but now she was learning the truth of it. Her peace of mind was gone, chased away by foreign emotions and strange feelings. It had happened so quickly, and that was the amazing thing. But it had happened, and now she was a totally different girl inside.

When she went down to the sitting-room she found Stella on the sofa, talking animatedly with Martin, who had closed the book he had been reading. There was a tense expression on his face that reminded Linda for all the world of a trapped animal, and she heard him sigh with relief when she appeared in the doorway. Stella shook her head slowly when she saw Linda, and got abruptly to her feet and left the room.

'Phew!' Martin said, getting to his feet. 'That was like the third degree a criminal gets. I'm going to have to be very careful in future not to get caught alone in a room with Stella.'

'But she's a very lovely girl. Isn't she your type?'

'She isn't, and that's definite,' Martin said briskly. 'By the way, your mother has returned, and Robert pounced on her the moment she walked in the door. He took her off into her private room, and they've been in there several minutes.'

'Oh! Thank you. Well, if Robert is keeping her busy, then I'd better see what Lucy is doing about tea.'

'I shall be ready to leave when you are,' he called after her as she left the room.

Linda walked past her mother's room with her ears keened, but she heard nothing of what was taking place inside. She giggled girlishly as she had a sudden picture in her mind of Robert down on one knee proposing to her mother.

'Well, you seem very happy,' Lucy said as Linda entered the kitchen.

The housekeeper was tall and thin, a widow of forty-nine who had been with Mavis Shelton long enough to be on sisterly terms with her. She had bright blue eyes that never missed anything, and now she was studying Linda closely and nodding significantly. She and Linda got along very well together. The housekeeper liked to gossip, but there was no malice in her.

'Shouldn't I be?' Linda retorted. 'I've got a good home that's very well managed by the staff of one, a smart, lovable mother, and a very good job.'

'You had all these things last week, and the week before that, but you weren't so full of beans. It's only come about since the new boarder arrived. I smell romance in the air.'

'Really? Is that what romance smells like? I thought it was tea you were preparing.' Linda spoke gravely, and Lucy shook her head.

'I hope it lasts for you, Linda,' the housekeeper said. 'It's the best thing in the world for a girl like you.'

'What is?'

'Marriage to a good man,' came the plain reply.

'Well, I live in hopes of finding a good man,' Linda said.

'You'll know him when he arrives,' she was told, 'and I shouldn't be at all surprised if that time is nearer to hand than you think. But you'd better take a word of warning. Watch Dr. Ingram. She isn't to be trusted with any man, and I'm telling you. If you are setting any store in this new doctor, then you'd better let him know as soon as possible. If you show him your icy side, then he'll go straight into Stella's arms.'

'You're just like my mother,' Linda said breathlessly. 'It must be because you're always with her. You read the most significant things into nothing. Really, Lucy, you ought to be ashamed of yourself. Martin is nothing but a stranger in this house. We've got to make the man feel at home, haven't we?'

'Not if it's too much of an effort,' a voice said from the doorway, and Linda spun around to see Martin standing there, a tight smile on his lips and a strange light in his eyes. 'Sorry, but I wasn't deliberately eavesdropping. I heard your mother calling you from her room, and I knew you were in here.' He smiled and backed out of the doorway, and before Linda could move she heard him going up the stairs.

By the time she reached the hall he had disappeared, and she went to her mother's room with a dragging hurt in her heart. She wouldn't have wanted him to hear those flippant words for anything in the world. But words were like arrows, and could not be called back, and they had the same hurtful quality, as she had seen by the expression in his eyes as he turned away.

Mavis Shelton was standing just inside her room, and the door was ajar. Linda swallowed her regret as she tapped at the door and went in. She was brought up short by the expression on her mother's face.

'Mother, are you all right?' she exclaimed,

and hurried to Mrs. Shelton's side.

'Yes, dear, don't fuss. I've had a shock, but it's nothing to worry about.'

'Oh!' Linda was recalling that Robert had been in here a few minutes earlier. So he had proposed! She waited for her mother to give her the details.

'You'll never guess, my dear,' Mrs. Shelton said excitedly. 'I shall have to sit down before I fall down. Never in all my days would I have imagined such a thing.'

'What is it, Mother? Robert was in here just now. What did he have to say to you?'

'He proposed to me!' Mrs. Shelton sat down, her blue eyes large and wondering. 'He wants to marry me, Linda. And I never guessed in all these years that he had any feelings at all for me.'

'And did you accept the proposal?' Linda asked gently.

'But of course I couldn't give him an immediate answer. It's taken my breath away. He says I've got to think calmly about it, and let him know as soon as I'm certain one way or another.'

'How do you feel about him, Mother?'

'I'm very fond of him, Linda, and I don't mind telling you.' There was a mixture of emotions in Mrs. Shelton's eyes. 'He's been a very close friend, but I never even guessed that he thought more than that about me. It's such a shock.'

Linda smiled, but there was trembling hope inside her. If her mother would be happy with Robert Pearce, then she would be pleased to see her remarry, but would Robert become heavy-handed after the marriage? He had mentioned that he wanted the house to cease being a home from home for unattached members of St. Margaret's medical staff. Would the changes stop there? She wondered how she could broach the subject to her mother without admitting that Robert had previously spoken to her about his proposal.

'Mother, if you married Robert,

would you continue to run this house on its present lines?'

'Of course, dear.' Mrs. Shelton stared at her daughter with surprise dawning in her eyes. 'Whatever made you ask that?'

'Perhaps Robert wouldn't approve.'

'I'll have to talk over details with him, of course. But I feel sure he would want me to go on with my interests. I don't think I could give it up. Anyway, where would our boarders go? They look upon this place as their home.'

'Well, I hope you will make the right decision, Mother,' Linda said, 'and if you decide to accept, then I hope you will be very happy.'

'Thank you, dear. I knew you would accept it like that.' Mrs. Shelton put her arms around Linda and hugged her. 'I was worried about your reactions, but you're a sensible girl. I think we will all be very happy together.'

'Then you are inclined to accept?' Linda demanded.

'I don't really know yet, dear. I must

have time to think it over, and not a word to anyone until I've decided.'

'I shan't breathe a word,' Linda said with a smile. 'I must say you've taken the wind out of my sails with this news. I can imagine how you must be feeling.'

'But work must go on,' Mrs. Shelton said, her tones becoming firm. 'It's almost tea-time. I stayed out longer than I had anticipated, and Robert caught me when I came in. I don't know if I'm on my head or my heels. I expect Lucy is fuming because I haven't been here to help.'

'Of course she isn't. I've just come out of the kitchen, and anyway, you know that Lucy never gets bad-tempered over anything. Really, Mother, you do create tension for yourself. No wonder you haven't been feeling on top of the world lately.'

'But I'm right up there at the top now, dear. Oh, I must have time to think. My poor head is whirling so, and I feel all bubbly inside.'

'You'd better sit down for a few

moments. I'll go and help Lucy with the tea. That's an order, Mother. I want you to take things easy. No fluttering around until I've gone off to the hospital.'

'All right, dear.' Mrs. Shelton sat down at the big desk.

'Now I'll go and fetch you a cup of tea, and after that you'll feel more like your old self. Perhaps Robert should have given you some inkling of his feelings before this. It's been quite a shock for you.'

Linda left the room and went into the kitchen. 'Mother wants a cup of tea, Lucy,' she said.

'So she's back. Is she all right? You look a bit worried.' The housekeeper was a kindly woman. 'Or is it that Martin overheard your words?' She laughed. 'Don't take that to heart. You won't have any trouble getting around him. I've seen it in his eyes, and he hasn't been here hardly more than a day.'

'You're talking nonsense,' Linda

retorted. 'Is the tea made? Mother is all excited about something or other. I should have gone out with her this afternoon.'

She poured a cup of tea and took it along to her mother's room. Mrs. Shelton was still seated at the desk, but she was dabbing at her eyes with a handkerchief, and Linda felt a pang of alarm.

'What on earth are you crying about?' she asked.

'It's nothing, dear, just an overflow of emotion. This has been quite a shock, and now I'm just beginning to realise what an acceptance would mean. My whole life would change overnight, wouldn't it? And I've got so used to everything the way it is. I don't think I could face it, Linda.'

'But you mustn't concern yourself with that kind of thing,' Linda told her gently. 'Forget the future and the past and concentrate upon your own feelings. That's the only way to arrive at your decision. You must be fair to

Robert, and don't let anything but your emotions sway you.'

'I know, dear.' Mrs. Shelton took the tea and began to sip it.

4

Helping to prepare the tea in her mother's place, Linda had little time in which to think about Martin. But she was dreading his appearance at tea, and when it was time to call down the boarders she was tempted to skip the meal and go into her room until it was time to leave for the hospital. But Martin appeared on the landing before she could get away, and he came down towards her, followed closely by Stella.

Linda stared at his face for some indication of his feelings. Her words must have sounded harsh and unkind to him, and perhaps he was already doubting her show of friendship. She didn't want that. She was nourishing the most tender feelings for him, and nothing must come along to change his ideas. She had sensed that he took to her, but those few words to put Lucy off had hurt him. He might lose confidence in her, and once he started doubting her motives there could be no chance for her.

But he smiled as he reached her side, and Linda felt relief well up inside her. While he and Stella went into the dining-room Linda went back into the kitchen, and she helped Lucy with the dishes. Glancing through the service hatch, she saw that Stella was seated beside Martin, and her heart seemed turned to stone when she saw how animatedly he was talking to the girl.

Mrs. Shelton came into the kitchen, and tried to shoo Linda away. Linda glanced at her watch, and saw that it was later than she had imagined. She would have to get her tea now. She went around to the dining-room, and as she took a seat at the far end of the long table, Stella glanced triumphantly at her.

None of the other boarders had arrived yet, and Stella was making the most of her unexpected monopoly of the new boarder's attention. Then Robert came into the room, and he sat down beside Linda. He was in obvious high spirits, and he smiled fondly at Linda as he caught her eye.

'Have you spoken to your mother recently?' he half-whispered.

'Yes.' Linda nodded. 'She told me about your proposal.'

'How do you think she's taking it?' Anxiety showed in his brown eyes.

'It's hard to tell with Mother. She's shocked at the moment, but tomorrow her mind will be clear again, and she'll soon let you know.'

'You haven't tried to influence her one way or another?'

'Certainly not. I told you this morning, Robert, that it was none of my business. I wouldn't try to interfere in my mother's life, unless I thought she would be making a bad mistake.'

'And you don't think that accepting my proposal would be a mistake for her?'

'No.' Linda smiled at the relief which

showed in his eyes. 'I think you're a very nice person, Robert, and Mother would have to look a long way to find another man as acceptable. But of course her feelings count for much, and the decision is entirely hers to make.'

'Thank you, Linda.' He glanced along the table, wondering if their words had been overheard. Stella was looking at them, smiling, happy with the situation.

'What on earth are you two whispering about?' the girl demanded. 'You're not planning to elope, are you?'

Linda smiled despite her feelings, and she saw that Martin was laughing. But there was still an awkwardness in the atmosphere that she sensed, and it didn't sit well with her. She was glad when Colin Lambert came in, followed shortly by Philip Norris.

Later, when it was time for her to leave, she looked into the sitting-room to see if Martin was ready to go with her. She found him with Stella, laughing at something she had said.

They looked up as Linda walked into the room, and Martin got immediately to his feet, excusing himself, leaving Stella staring after him with a determined expression on her lovely face.

'Are you ready to go?' he asked as he reached Linda.

She nodded, not trusting herself to speak. She was feeling shaky inside, and her throat seemed constricted. They went out to the garage, and Linda found her hands were trembling as she unlocked the car.

'You can drive me to the hospital,' she said, and her voice sounded stilted in her ears.

'Want to find out if I can really drive?' he teased, taking the keys from her.

'Well, there is something in that.' She smiled, and he nodded.

'All right, I'll put her through her paces. But I admit that I'm not a mad driver. I'll bring the car back safe and sound, and right on the dot of ten.'

They got into the car, and Linda felt strange sitting in the front passenger seat. Martin switched on and started the car, and when he moved off she realised that he was a good driver.

They travelled in silence most of the way, and she could hear Martin humming softly. Her chance to explain what she meant by those words he had overheard in the kitchen was gone, she realised as the hospital came in sight. She should have spoken to him immediately after it happened.

'You know,' he said as he turned into the hospital car-park, 'Stella might be a clinging vine and all that, but she's good fun. She knows how to make a fellow feel happy.'

'I said there was no harm in her,' Linda replied. 'I count Stella as a good friend.' She opened the door of the car when he halted. 'I'll look for you at ten.'

'I'll be here, and thanks again for letting me take the car. I appreciate your trust in me.'

Linda smiled and got out. She waved good-bye, then went slowly into the hospital.

In a way it was a relief to get to work, she told herself as she donned her white coat and took up the list that awaited her.

She went along to the wards to check upon the various patients, and by the time she had finished the essential visits the evening was half over. Then she went back to her office and handled some of the eternal paperwork that was the bugbear of her life.

At ten she left the hospital, and when she reached the car-park Martin was there waiting for her. He was sitting in the front passenger seat, and he smiled when Linda got in behind the steering wheel.

'Well, how did it go?' he asked.

'The same as usual. There's never a spare minute.' She glanced obliquely at him as she started the car. 'How's your evening gone? It's rather early to leave two friends, isn't it?'

'Not really. Tom has just gone on duty, and they knew I was coming to pick you up. But we had a nice time, talking about the old days. Isn't it strange how people always find the past worth talking about? I suppose it's because we're growing older, and like to think of lost youth.'

'Do you want to go home now?' she asked, and there was a catch in her voice despite her efforts to remain calm.

'You must be tired,' he replied quickly. 'There's nothing much to do but go for a drive. I'm ready to find my bed, and I'm sure you must be.'

'No,' she said slowly. 'I'm thinking of taking a drive for an hour. Would you like me to drop you off at the house on my way?'

'Do you want me to come along?' he challenged.

'I'm sure you won't be any trouble.' Linda smiled. 'But you may have some doubts about that after what you overheard me saying to Lucy. Do I have to explain that?'

'No.' He smiled and relaxed. 'I could tell that she was being nosey. I would have said exactly the same thing in your place.'

Linda could have kissed him in her relief, and she drove out of the car-park feeling elated.

She headed out of town and followed a narrow road into the dark countryside. Martin was silent for the most part, but she could tell that the tension which had existed between them after her words with Lucy earlier in the evening had gone. She let her thoughts drift, but the subject was always the same. She could not get her mind off this man at her side.

'Tomorrow is Sunday,' he suddenly remarked, jerking her back from her mental ramble. 'What are you doing with yourself? Do you have to go on duty?'

'No, it's my day of rest,' she told him hopefully. 'What are your plans?'

'I'll do some studying, I expect. I shall be following the rest of you on Monday, and that will put a certain amount of curtailment upon my leisure activities.'

Linda wanted to ask him out for a drive, but could not bring herself to broach the matter. She drove on in silence, for a while, then glanced at her watch and saw that it was time to think of starting back.

'It's getting late,' Martin said, catching her movement. 'But I suppose you'll have a lie-in tomorrow morning.'

'I'm usually up quite early,' she replied.

'Then you might as well stop the car for a bit.' There was sudden tension in his voice, she noticed, and her heart seemed to miss a beat.

'All right,' she agreed, and wondered why she was not shocked by the knowledge that she hoped he would take advantage of the situation. A week ago she would have been horrified by her own actions, but now, after meeting him, she was impatient to feel his arms around her. She saw a gateway ahead and slowed the car, running on to the verge and parking. As she switched off the engine and the headlights she felt a fluttering in her breast, and her hands were trembling.

'You know something?' he said, his face just a pale blur in the dashboard light. 'I have a strange feeling about you. I don't ordinarily bother with girls, as you probably know. I never did find the time for them, and must say that they never seemed worth the bother it took to keep them happy. But you seem to be different. Perhaps it's because you're one of the few girls I've met who doesn't want to throw herself into my arms and start making plans for an early marriage.'

'Do girls normally want to do that?' she asked, her throat constricting. She was aching to get close to him.

'Well, that's the way of things, isn't it?' He laughed, and shifted his position suddenly. 'But you seem to have no interest whatever in the opposite sex, and perhaps that's what is pushing at me. Perhaps my pride is being challenged. But I have a pretty strong urge to kiss you. Doesn't that sound crazy to you? We haven't known each other more than a matter of hours, and this urge goes deeper than any man's desire to kiss a pretty girl. There's something about you that attracts me, and I'm only too aware of it.'

'That's the way it goes sometimes,' Linda said slowly, hoping that he would make some move towards her. 'But you're being unusually frank, aren't you?'

'Just because I want you to fully understand my motives,' he replied, and the next instant he had leaned across to her and found her lips with his firm mouth.

Linda gasped, and stiffened instinctively, but he remained against her, one hand touching the back of her neck. She felt incredible sensations coming to life inside her, and slowly relaxed against him. Time seemed to stand still. There was nothing in the surrounding darkness but his presence, and the strangely comforting feeling of his lips against hers. She put up her arms and slid her hands around his neck, and he pulled her tightly into his strong embrace. The kiss went on and on.

When he finally drew away he sighed deeply. Linda remained perfectly still, her hands still touching his neck. For a moment there was silence, and Linda had never felt so contented in her whole life.

'Well,' he said with a sharp intake of breath, 'I suppose that puts paid to what must have been the start of a very promising friendship.'

'I wanted you to do that,' she said honestly.

'Wonders never cease!' He was tense now. 'You really mean that? You wanted me to kiss you?'

'Why else would I have suggested a drive after a long evening at the hospital?' she retorted. 'I knew instinctively from the first moment I saw you that my feelings would be in some danger of changing. I have never behaved like this with anyone. I'm shocked by my behaviour, but it was worth it.'

He did not reply, and she wondered what was going on in his mind. Then he came towards her again, and put his arms around her.

'Might as well hang for a sheep as a lamb,' he said, and she thrilled as he kissed her.

She was astonished when next she glanced at her watch. The time was ten minutes past twelve.

'Oh, heavens!' he exclaimed when she told him. 'What will your mother have to say? You left the hospital two hours ago.'

'She'll guess that you've taken me for a drive,' Linda replied quickly.

'I won't have that,' he retorted with a laugh. 'You took me for a drive.'

'That's true, and I'll make that perfectly plain to my mother.'

'We'd better be going now, anyway,' he resumed with a reluctant sigh. 'What did you say you would be doing tomorrow?'

'Anything you wish,' Linda told him happily.

'We'll talk about it in the morning.' He moved back to his side of the car and stretched. 'That's if you'll be awake before noon. It's almost an hour's drive back to town, isn't it?'

'No, thank goodness,' Linda replied. 'I took the longest way out I knew. We can get back in fifteen minutes.'

'Well, I'll be — !' He stared at her. 'So you really took me for a ride tonight. I've been the victim of a dastardly plan.'

'You haven't come to any harm,' she retorted, and he laughed.

They drove back to Redford in fifteen minutes. When they went into the house Linda was very tense, afraid that her mother might have waited up for her, but all was silent and still, and they went softly to their respective rooms.

As she stumbled sleepily into bed, Linda thrilled to the memory of Martin's strong arms and gentle lips, and she drifted quickly into sleep with an easy mind . . .

In the morning she awoke with the

feeling that something important was about to happen, and lying in that blissful state of dreaming between sleeping and waking, she tried to figure out what it was. Then she came fully awake. It had already happened. Martin had kissed her! She breathed deeply as the memory came back, and the emotions that filtered through her were almost too sharp to bear.

She arose quickly and dressed, wondering what Martin would want to do during the day. They could go out together in the afternoon and for the evening. She didn't expect her mother would want to go out — there would be too much upon her mind.

Linda smiled gently as she thought about her mother. What would be the sequel to Robert's proposal? Would he become her stepfather? She shook her head as she went slowly down the stairs to the kitchen. Events were moving fast, and in a household where time had seemed to stand still for a very great number of years.

Lucy was busy at the stove, and the smell of frying bacon reminded Linda she'd had no supper. Lucy gave her a keen glance, and jerked a thumb towards the teapot.

'Have a nice time last night?' the housekeeper asked. 'You look positively rosy this morning.'

'We went for a short drive after Martin picked me up at ten,' Linda replied as she poured tea. 'Has Mother come down yet?'

'No. I'd like to know what she's sickening for. Last evening she was like a mother hen gone broody. I've never seen her so nervous. Robert asked her out for a drink, but she wouldn't go. She said she had too much on her mind to enjoy herself. Spring is nearly over, but this house seems to be affected by its presence. I've heard of lambs feeling the time of year, but you and your mother are both old enough to know better.'

'I don't know what you're driving at, Lucy,' Linda said firmly. 'Sometimes I wonder if you can follow your own reasoning. What are you trying to say?'

'Now don't come all that innocence stuff with me, young woman,' Lucy said. 'I wasn't born yesterday, and if you are contemplating getting serious about Dr. Crossley, then let him know it before Stella gets her claws into him. She was really working on him yesterday.'

Linda glanced towards the door, remembering that her words had been overheard before, and she smiled as she sat down at the table to drink her tea. She could hear someone moving around on the floor above, and guessed that her mother was about to appear.

'Who's on duty today?' Lucy demanded. 'Your mother forgot to enquire last night. That's unusual for her. She's getting lackadaisical in her old age.'

'Robert and Philip will be on duty,' Linda told her.

'That means Stella will be hanging around the house all day, waiting to pounce on Dr. Crossley. You'll have to get in quick if you want to catch him, my girl.'

'Lucy, you do have queer ideas on how romances should be conducted.'

'All's fair in love and war,' the housekeeper quoted with a smile.

Lucy finished her tea and began to collect the cutlery to take into the dining-room. As she piled them on the tray her mother came into the kitchen, and one glance was enough to tell Linda that her mother had slept badly.

'Mother,' she said, 'you've been lying awake half the night. That's really too bad of you.'

'I couldn't help it, dear. It's such a big decision to make. I wish it hadn't happened now.'

'What's this I've been missing?' Lucy demanded suspiciously. 'What are you holding back from me?'

'It's nothing at all, Lucy. Let me take those things into the dining-room, Linda. There's no need for you to do my work. This is your day of rest, and you must take things easy. Did you have a nice time last night? When you weren't home by eleven I guessed that you and Martin had gone for a drive. What time did you get in?'

'About a quarter past twelve,' Linda said.

'And were you very busy at the hospital during the evening, dear?'

'About the usual.' Linda picked up the tray although her mother tried to take it. 'You sit down there and have a nice cup of tea. I'll lay the table.' She glanced at her watch. 'They'll be coming down very shortly.'

'Well, everything's ready this end,' Lucy said firmly, her eyes twinkling. 'It's a good job I wind up my alarm clock on a Saturday evening.'

As she left the kitchen Linda heard footsteps on the stairs, and she looked up eagerly. But it was Robert descending, and his face told her that he'd spent an uneasy night. He beckoned to her as their glances met, and she smiled and waited for him to join her.

'Has your mother given any indication of the way her thoughts are turning?' he asked in a hoarse whisper.

'Do you think there's any chance that she'll accept?'

'I wouldn't know about that, Robert, but you've certainly given her something to think about. She hardly slept last night, and I do believe it will take her several days to recover from the shock of your proposal. It won't be until she has recovered that she'll be able to think rationally. I'm afraid you'll just have to find the patience to wait.'

'Has she asked your advice?' he pursued.

'No, and I wouldn't presume to say anything. It's a decision she'll have to make entirely on her own.'

'I half wish I hadn't been so rash now,' he went on. 'It may cause a lot of worry for all concerned. Is breakfast ready?'

'Yes. I'll tell Lucy you're down.' Linda smiled as she went into the dining-room and laid the table.

Her mother came in with a plate piled high with slices of bread and butter, and Robert looked a little sheepish as he turned to greet her. Linda hid her smile and hurriedly left them alone. She went back into the kitchen for Robert's breakfast and caught Lucy at the service hatch, peeping through a narrow opening.

'Lucy,' she reproved, 'that isn't done by the best staff.'

The housekeeper turned quickly, quite unabashed. 'There's something going on in this house, or my instincts are playing me false for the first time in my life. What's it all about, Linda? Don't be mean.'

'I'm afraid I don't understand,' Linda replied, laughing.

'Your mother is acting like a schoolgirl and Robert Pearce is blushing like a youth. Has he proposed to her? I've had a feeling for years that something like that was in the wind.'

'Lucy, you're the limit! What would Mother say if she heard you talking like that?'

'Don't try to pull the wool over my eyes, young woman,' came the sharp retort. 'I'll tell you this much, it will be a sad day for this house if your mother is foolish enough to accept.'

Linda didn't reply. She waited for Lucy to serve out Robert's breakfast, then she carried it out of the kitchen and along the corridor to the dining-room instead of using the service hatch. She was thoughtful as she entered the room. Robert was seated in his customary place at the table, and her mother was standing near by with a faraway look in her pale blue eyes.

'I'll get the tea,' Mrs. Shelton said hurriedly, pulling herself together. 'What am I thinking of? I don't know if I'm on my head or my heels this morning.'

'Well, Robert?' Linda demanded when her mother had left the room. 'Has she reached a decision yet?'

'No.' He shook his head. 'I keep telling her there's no hurry for her to decide, but the waiting is killing me.'

Philip Norris came into the room, smiling, which was rare for him, and as he sat down at the table he glanced at

Linda. There was unaccustomed humour in his dark eyes.

'Your mother is in a flap this morning,' he commented. 'She just passed me in the hall, and I do believe she was talking to herself.'

'She's passing through a personal crisis,' Linda said and Robert glared warningly at her.

'I see.' Norris glanced at Robert, but said nothing more.

Linda walked to the service hatch and rapped upon it. Lucy opened it, and passed through Philip's breakfast. The housekeeper was smiling, but Linda didn't query it. She saw her mother in the kitchen, standing by the table and staring vacantly into space.

'I'll have my breakfast now, Lucy, please,' Linda said, 'and you'd better give me Mother's, then send her around, will you?'

'I'll be glad to,' Lucy said. 'I want her out of my way this morning. She's no earthly use in here.'

Linda fetched her own breakfast, and

119

saw her mother leaving the kitchen with a plate in her hand. As she sat down at the table Mrs. Shelton came in through the doorway, holding her breakfast.

'We had that service hatch put into the wall at great expense, Mother,' Linda said severely. 'Why don't you use it?'

'Sorry, dear, I was thinking.'

'Must be the weather,' Norris remarked. 'It's a lovely day out there, and I've got to be cooped up in the hospital until six.'

'You're lucky,' Robert grumbled. 'I shall be there until late this evening.'

As she ate, Linda found herself glancing occasionally at the door, looking for Martin to appear. Her heart lifted when she heard a sound in the hall, but Stella appeared instead of Martin, and she looked down at her plate after greeting the girl.

Stella was in good spirits. She rapped at the service hatch to summon her breakfast, and came to sit beside Linda to eat it.

'What's everyone doing today?' she

demanded. Her blue eyes swivelled to Linda's face. 'Are you going anywhere in that car of yours? Where's Martin? Isn't he down yet?'

The front door slammed at that moment, and Mrs. Shelton leapt to her feet.

'Who on earth is that at this hour?' she demanded, leaving the table, but before she could reach the door Martin appeared in the doorway.

'Good morning,' he greeted. 'I've been for a stroll. It is a beautiful morning, or it was when I first went out, but it's beginning to cloud over a little.'

'Why didn't you call me?' Stella demanded. 'I like nothing better than a good stroll before breakfast, but I don't like going alone, and there are no early morning strollers in this house.'

Martin smiled but made no reply, and his eyes were on Linda, who smiled at him and got to her feet. She went to fetch his breakfast, and although Stella made a great show of pulling out the chair next to her, he sat opposite. Linda put his meal before him and he thanked her warmly.

'Are you ready to leave, Philip?' Robert demanded at length. 'Time is getting away. I don't expect to be very busy on a day like this, but one never knows.' He got to his feet and Norris arose. Robert glanced at Mrs. Shelton. 'I shall be home at twelve-thirty for lunch. What about you, Philip?'

'Same time,' Norris replied, and they took their leave.

As they left the room Colin Lambert appeared. 'Good morning,' the young houseman called, going for his breakfast. 'What are you doing today, Stella? Would you like to come for a drive? I've managed to borrow Neil Warren's car. He'll be on duty all day. I don't like driving alone, so what about it?'

'I don't think so, Colin,' Stella replied, her eyes upon Martin, and Linda could almost read the girl's mind. Stella was hoping that Martin would be available at some time during the day.

Linda took a deep breath and spoke to Martin. 'Mother won't be going out with me at all today,' she said, glancing at her mother. 'So shall we take a picnic lunch and go off into the country?'

Stella jerked her head around to stare at Linda.

Martin looked up and smiled. 'I was wondering if I dared ask you to waste so much time with me today,' he replied. 'But if you have nothing better to do, then I shall thoroughly enjoy a day out.'

Linda smiled her relief, and she saw that her mother was nodding energetically in agreement. 'Shall we ask Lucy to make up a picnic basket?'

'It's a deal,' Martin said. 'When shall we leave?'

'About ten.' Linda glanced at her watch. 'It will give me time to get ready.'

'I hope you'll have a very nice time,' Mrs. Shelton said, getting to her feet. 'I'll attend to the picnic basket myself.'

'Why don't we make up a foursome?'

Stella demanded quickly. 'I can travel with Colin in his car and we can rendezvous at some spot.'

'Will you come with me?' Colin demanded.

'Yes, all right. I feel like a day out.'

'But not with us,' Linda said firmly. 'You're not going to be a spoilsport, Stella.'

'All right.' The girl sighed good-naturedly. 'I know when I'm beaten. I'll go with Colin.'

Linda got to her feet, filled with urgency now. She smiled at Martin as she left the room to get ready, and her heart was filled with overwhelming joy as she made her way up the stairs to her room. The long day was stretching far ahead of them, and most of its sunny hours would be theirs alone. She couldn't get out of the house quick enough. It must be love, she told herself tenderly. No other feelings could have been so ecstatic.

5

With the picnic basket stowed away in the boot of the car and Martin in the front passenger seat, Linda felt on top of the world as she drove out of town. The sun was shining brightly and there were few clouds in the deep-blue sky. The countryside was green and luxuriant, with the hedgerows filled colourfully, and Linda wanted to sing at the top of her voice.

At her side, Martin sat relaxed, gazing around with interest, and she could tell by the expression on his face that he was thoroughly enjoying himself. They were both silent for the most part, content to drink in the scenery and to enjoy the warm day.

'I've just had a dreadful thought,' Martin suddenly remarked.

'What was that?' she asked. 'Haven't forgotten something, have you?'

'No.' He laughed. 'I just had a picture of me sitting in my room studying. Fancy doing something like that on a perfectly beautiful day like this!'

'It is dreadful,' she agreed. 'Let's make a bargain, shall we? Let's take advantage of every beautiful day this summer, duty permitting, and get out in the car.'

'I'm all for it. I'm only just realising what I've been missing all these years. But of course it rather depends upon the company one keeps, doesn't it?' He eyed her questioningly and there was a gentle expression on his face.

'I've got no complaints about my company,' she replied ardently.

'And the same goes for me.' He spoke in low tones, and Linda glanced at him, her eyes shining, her heart beating faster than ever. He leaned sideways, and she could not move because she was driving fast along a straight road. He put an arm along the back of her seat, and she could feel his breath on her cheek.

'I lay awake last night for some time,' he admitted slowly. 'Kissing you disturbed me greatly, and I'm wondering if it was just a combination of the night itself and my thoughts. Was it something inside me that made me feel flirtatious? I've never been like that with any girl. I was hoping you'd ask me out today because I wanted the chance to find out for certain.' His lips touched her cheek, and Linda trembled, her hands clutching convulsively at the steering wheel.

'Martin,' she gasped, 'you'll have us off the road.'

'Then stop the car. I must know the answer now.'

She glanced in the mirror and applied the brake, and when the car halted on the verge she switched off and turned to him.

When their lips met she shuddered, and went limp against him, clinging with all her strength. He was breathing deeply, seized with unaccustomed passion, and the silence in the car pressed about them like a physical force.

'Oh, Martin,' she whispered when he released her slowly. 'What are you doing to me?'

'Do you feel it, too?' he demanded, and his eyes were alight with emotion.

'Kiss me again,' she pleaded.

He did so, slowly and tenderly, and Linda felt that she was drifting ecstatically into a new world of delight. No one had ever made her feel like this, she told herself, opening her eyes as he released her. She saw that he was smiling, and she made no move to resume driving.

'Well,' she said, 'was it just the night and you? Or did I have anything to do with that feeling you had?'

'It was you, without a doubt,' he said a trifle unsteadily. 'Oh, Linda, I've never been so mixed up before. We're still almost strangers, aren't we? And yet I feel as if I've known you for ever, and I don't ever want to lose sight of you.' He paused and sighed. 'Don't I sound like a love-struck youth out on his first date?'

'If you do, then I'm in the same

boat,' she replied slowly. 'Perhaps I shouldn't tell you this, Martin, but it's how I feel, and I think you should know.'

'I knew instinctively when I first saw you that you would figure importantly in my life,' he went on. 'No girl ever attracted me before.'

'My experience entirely,' she replied, trying to keep her tones even.

His hand on the back of her seat kept stroking her neck, and Linda leaned towards him. They kissed again, and minutes passed before he released her.

'Perhaps we'd better drive on,' he said unsteadily. 'It is rather early in the day to start cuddling in a car. We have no shame, Linda.'

She smiled up at him, but made no effort to move.

'Just kiss me once more,' she pleaded, and he did.

When she drove on, her heart was beating like a steam hammer. This was definitely love, she told herself tensely, and it was better than the nagging doubts she had felt on that first day when Stella had started working her wiles. But she knew she didn't have to fear Stella's rivalry now. Martin was well beyond the clutches of the girl.

The rest of the morning seemed to fly away, and it was time for lunch when Linda stopped the car on a heath. There were other cars parked around, and she drove slowly along a bumpy track until she found a secluded spot.

When she parked Martin helped her get out the hamper, and they ate in the sunshine, and drank coffee from the flask her mother had provided. Afterwards they stretched out on the car rug and soaked up the sun.

Linda drifted into a light sleep, and did not move until her eyes fluttered open. The first thing she saw was Martin's face peering at her. He was lying at her side, propped up on his elbows. He smiled when he saw she was awake.

'Hello,' he said. 'So you've come back to me.'

'Have I been asleep long?' she asked. Her face was hot from the rays of the sun, and her dress was almost burning to her touch. 'Ouch, I'm almost roasted.'

'I've kept most of the sun from your face.'

He put an arm across her, encircling her waist and drawing her close to him. She closed her eyes and tilted her face to him, and his mouth was firm against her lips.

'Do you feel like going on somewhere else?' he asked at length, leaning away from her to look into her eyes.

'No, do you?'

'Not at all. I'm quite content to stay here kissing you, although we can't spend every moment together just kissing.'

'Why not?' she demanded, and they both laughed. He squeezed her, and she sighed contentedly. 'I wish today would never end,' she said wistfully.

'That's not the right attitude to take,' he replied severely. 'There'll be other days, other outings. But life goes on, remember, and it doesn't help to want to stay still. Look ahead, Linda.'

'All right, I'll do that,' she replied with a smile. 'But I feel right now I shouldn't be able to sit still five minutes at a time.'

He bent and kissed her gently on the mouth, and she put her arms around his neck. They remained motionless, in silence, for a long time, and then Linda sighed and glanced at her watch. The afternoon was almost gone, and they should start thinking about returning home.

She was reluctant to leave, but the afternoon was gone and their day had come to an end. They put away the hamper and climbed into the car, and Linda caught a glimpse of her face in the rear view mirror as she switched on the engine. She had caught the sun through sleeping out in it, and her eyes seemed unnaturally bright. They were filled with the glorious shine of inner fire, and looking at Martin, she saw a similar expression in his eyes.

On the drive back to town she was silent, and Martin lolled in his seat. The windows were wide open, and the sound of the tyres swishing on the road was soothing. Linda felt as if she had known Martin all her life. That was the most peculiar aspect about the whole affair. He didn't seem like a stranger. And she didn't need to question her feelings or to be told that she was in love.

When they reached the outskirts of Redford, Linda slowed the car. Martin glanced at her, a smile on his face.

'You'd better let yourself cool down a little before we go home,' he said. 'Your eyes are shining and your colour is scarlet. I'm sure that anyone looking at you will be able to tell what your feelings are.'

'I'm not ashamed of how I feel. I don't care who guesses. I've had a perfectly wonderful day, and I feel on top of the world.'

'I'm glad.' He reached out and squeezed

her hand. 'I was looking forward to starting work tomorrow, but now my only concern seems to be to get away somewhere with you. Isn't that a completely irresponsible way to think?'

'Emotions are a bit overwhelming sometimes,' she replied.

When they reached home Linda drove the car straight into the garage, and Martin paused before reaching out to open the door.

'You drove in here as if you never intended taking the car out again,' he said gently. 'What are you going to do this evening?'

'I was rather hoping that you'd ask me,' she replied. 'Have you any suggestions?'

'A walk around town,' he said eagerly. 'It would round off a perfectly wonderful day.'

'I'm all for it,' Linda told him. They got out of the car and she collected the hamper. 'I have rather neglected Mother today,' Linda observed guiltily as they entered the house. 'She was extremely good when I sprang it upon her this morning. But I think she knows how it is with me. She's been trying to throw us together from the moment you arrived, or didn't you notice?'

'All mothers do the best they can for their daughters,' Martin said. 'Isn't the house silent? You can tell it's a Sunday afternoon. I'm glad we've been out all day.'

Linda went into the kitchen while Martin went up to his room, and she found Lucy there, preparing tea. The housekeeper smiled at her and nodded her head knowingly.

'I don't have to ask if you've enjoyed yourself,' she said. 'I'm glad the weather kept fine for you.'

Linda undid the picnic hamper and began to unpack it. Lucy helped her with the dirty plates and cups. 'Is Mother around? How has she been today?'

'Running around in circles all the time. I'd like to know what it is she's got on her mind. Won't you tell me, Linda?'

'I expect she'll tell us all about it when she's ready,' Linda replied with a smile.

'She went to lie down, but I've heard her feet overhead, so she hasn't been asleep. Stella and Colin aren't back yet. I feel sorry for that boy, traipsing around with her. She's only using him to pass her time, but he seems happy in her company.'

Linda dried her hands and left the kitchen, and saw her mother coming down the stairs. Mrs. Shelton waved cheerily and almost jumped down the remaining stairs.

'Linda, I'm so glad you're back,' she cried. 'I thought I heard Martin in his room but couldn't be sure. Did you have a nice time, dear?'

'Wonderful, Mother, but I do feel a little guilty. I usually take you for a drive on Sunday afternoons when I'm off duty.'

'Don't mention it, my dear. I wouldn't have been happy this afternoon, anyway. I've got too much on my mind. And you have spent far too much time in my company, you know. It's only right that you should get out and about with a nice young man. Did Martin enjoy himself?'

'He said he did.' Linda smiled as she recalled the day. 'Have you made any plans for this evening?'

'No, dear. There are one or two small jobs I want to catch up on. What was it you wanted to do? You'll be going out with Martin, of course.'

'If you don't want to go out, then I'll go with him.' Linda nodded slowly. She wanted to spend all her free time with him. 'Have you reached any decision upon that proposal yet?'

'No, dear. I just can't apply myself to the task. What shall I do?'

'Don't ask me, whatever you do.' Linda shook her head. 'I can't help you with that one, Mother, and you know it.'

'I wish Robert hadn't broached the subject,' Mrs. Shelton said.

Linda saw the kitchen door move ever so slightly, and put a restraining hand upon her mother's arm. She smiled as she indicated the kitchen.

'Lucy is just dying to know what's on your mind, Mother,' she said loudly. 'When are you going to tell her and put her out of her misery?'

The kitchen door opened and Lucy appeared, smiling.

'There's nothing to tell, yet,' Mrs. Shelton said, and hurried into the kitchen to help the housekeeper with tea.

Linda went up to her room and prepared to take a shower. As she went to the bathroom Martin emerged, and he smiled at her.

'All right for this evening?' he asked.

'Yes. Mother won't go out with me while there's a possibility you will want to take me out.'

'Then she'll never go out with you again,' he declared.

Linda smiled and went into the bathroom. She showered, and felt much refreshed as she dressed for the evening. When she went down the stairs tea was ready. Gerald Olley appeared from the sitting-room, almost bumping into Linda as she approached. He stepped aside for her, glancing twice at her radiant face, and nodded slowly to himself.

'I knew it would happen one day,' he said cheerfully.

'What's that?' Linda queried.

'What's happened to you over the past two days, my girl. But it's a good thing that I am old enough to be your father or Martin Crossley would have been much too late for you.'

They went into the dining-room together, and Martin was seated at the table, talking to Philip Norris.

'I don't believe I've ever seen you looking so lovely,' Norris remarked. 'Being out in the sun all day does wonders for you, Linda.'

'It's not being in the sun but her companion at the time,' Olley declared. 'What a pity I'm almost the wrong side of fifty.'

'You must have had your time,' Norris said firmly.

'I did, and I wasted my chances,'

139

Olley said slowly.

Tea was a light-hearted affair. Mrs. Shelton kept getting up from the table on the slightest pretext and running to the kitchen. She was obviously struggling with the decision she had been asked to make, and Linda felt sorry for her, but there was nothing she could do to help.

After tea, Linda began glancing frequently at her watch. They retired to the sitting-room, and the conversation turned naturally to hospitals and colleagues. It transpired that Martin knew several former colleagues of Philip Norris, and they had a good time discussing the merits and demerits of various nursing methods and treatments of chronic diseases.

As time went by Linda excused herself and went to her room to put the finishing touches to her make-up. The telephone rang as she was descending the stairs again, and she hurried to answer it. Robert spoke to her.

'Hello, Linda, glad to catch you and

not your mother. I just wanted to ask what the latest situation is. I know I'm a dashed nuisance, but the suspense is killing me.'

'I'm afraid I have to report no change, Robert,' she replied, and he thanked her profusely and apologised for being a nuisance. As she hung up, her mother appeared.

'Who was that, dear?' Mrs. Shelton enquired.

'Just Robert asking for a progress report.'

'Oh dear!' Mrs. Shelton paused and lifted a wavering hand to her head. 'What am I coming to?' she demanded. 'It's getting so I can't think straight.'

'Would you like to have a talk about it?' Linda asked.

'Have you got the time?' her mother asked anxiously.

'Martin is busy talking to Philip. I should think we've got plenty of time. Let's go into your room, Mother.'

Mrs. Shelton nodded and led the way. She sighed heavily as she closed the door behind Linda, and she went to seat herself behind the desk while Linda crossed to the window to peer out at the garden. There was silence, and then Mrs. Shelton began talking nervously.

'What shall I do, Linda?' she asked. 'I'm at my wits' end. It's no good saying I should calm down and think clearly. I'm past that.'

'Well, tell me what's in your mind, Mother,' Linda said gently. 'Perhaps I can help you into a decision. But I'm not going to sway you in any way. First of all, tell me your feelings for Robert. Are you in love with him?'

'Love?' her mother demanded with a little laugh. 'At my age?'

'Well, there are different kinds of love, Mother.' Linda spoke gently. 'How do you feel about him?'

'Well, I'm very fond of him, dear. That's to be expected after all these years I've known him.'

'Don't apologise for it, Mother. It's nothing to be ashamed of. Are your feelings strong enough to make you want to spend the rest of your life with him?'

'That's just it, I don't really know, and I can't see how I'm going to make up my mind. There are so many things to take into account. What happens if you suddenly decide to get married? You'll move out of the house, won't you? I shall be all alone then. On the other hand, Robert does have some funny little ways, and I might lose a great deal more of my freedom than I'd care to.'

'Poor Mother!' Linda said. 'You seem to have gone into it thoroughly, but the decision is yours. You should know better than I that some sacrifices have to be made in a marriage. It's up to you to weigh up the pros and cons and decide if you would be better off married to Robert or not. That's all I can say on the matter, and it doesn't help you one little bit, I know.'

'Thank you, dear, for being so understanding, but what shall I do? I was never a woman for making decisions. At one moment I feel that Robert is just the man for me, and that another marriage would be exactly what I need to round off my life, and then the doubts start coming. I just don't know what to do.'

'Try another track,' Linda suggested. 'Tell yourself that you won't marry Robert, and see what your feelings are, or do exactly the opposite and tell yourself that you will marry him. Then examine your feelings with the decision made. If you feel happy about it, then it will be the right one.'

Mrs. Shelton nodded, her face showing concentration. It would have seemed comical if she hadn't been so desperate. Linda sighed as she waited. Mrs. Shelton closed her eyes and pressed her hands together.

'I will marry Robert,' she said, and there was silence. For a few moments she remained motionless, almost in an attitude of prayer. Then she opened her eyes and stared at Linda. 'I don't feel any different,' she complained. 'Everything still seems mixed up. But wait a moment and let me try the opposite.' She closed her eyes again and said in tense tones: 'I won't marry Robert.'

Linda shook her head. She had no doubts about her feelings for Martin, and she began to think that her mother couldn't be in love with Robert or she would know without any doubt what she should do.

Mrs. Shelton opened her eyes then, and nodded slowly. 'I felt a distinct sadness,' she announced. 'So I would miss Robert if he left, which he would do if I rejected him. My mind is made up now. I will marry him.'

'Well, don't tell Robert yet,' Linda said happily. 'Think about it for a few hours, with the knowledge that you will accept in your mind. By the time he gets home this evening you should know for certain if you are making the right decision. Talk to Lucy about it now, if you like. It might help to have a few words with someone else, and Lucy is a kindly, sympathetic soul. I'm happy for you, Mother. I hope you will do the right thing, and if you marry Robert I hope you will be extremely happy.'

'Thank you, dear.' Mrs. Shelton put her arms around Linda and hugged her. 'And perhaps your turn will come before very long. You seem quite taken up with Martin, and he's a very nice person. He seems to like you, too.'

'Now you attend to your own affairs, Mother, and don't try your hand at match-making.' Linda smiled as she hugged her mother. 'I can do very well on my own account, you know.'

'I'm sure you can, dear, but I have been a bit worried about you. You're leaving marriage a bit late. I can understand that until now you haven't had much time for that sort of thing, but now you're settled in at St. Margaret's you should start getting interested in the opposite sex.'

'I'm getting interested all right,' Linda said. 'Now I must go. Martin is taking me for a walk this evening. I shan't be home too late. I feel tired already. Lying out in the sun is more tiring than a day's work.'

'Enjoy yourself, dear. I'm going to have a heart-to-heart talk with Lucy, but I'll keep the good news from everyone else until I've had a chance to talk to Robert. Good-bye for now.'

Linda kissed her mother's cheek, and she felt light-hearted as she left the little room. Life was like that, she told herself. One seemed to get into a rut for years, going about the same old rounds and not appearing to make very much progress, and then something happened to change everything, and life became happier and brighter.

She went into the sitting-room and found Martin sitting alone, waiting for her. He got to his feet when he saw her, big and powerful, smiling in relief.

'I thought you had deserted me,' he said. 'But Lucy told me you were in with your mother. Not getting a lecture about being in rather late last night, were you?'

'No.' Linda smiled. 'Mother wouldn't interfere with my life. She seems to think I have enough sense to run it how it should be done. She's been trying to arrive at a rather difficult decision all day, and it was wearing on her nerves. We've just had a long talk, and I think she'll be all right now.'

'Lucy kept hinting about something in the air,' he said. 'I don't know what she was getting at, but she seems to think it is all wrong.'

'Oh dear,' Linda said. 'Mother plans to talk to her about it, and if Lucy is against it and says so it might put Mother back where she started. Will you give me a few moments while I talk to Lucy?'

'Go right ahead,' he told her, sitting down again. 'The night is still young.'

She smiled appreciatively and went into the kitchen, and found Lucy seated at the table with a pack of playing cards.

'What on earth are you doing, Lucy?' she demanded. 'I didn't know you were a cardsharp.'

'I'm trying to get the future out of

them,' the housekeeper replied. She nodded slowly, and smiled thinly. 'You may laugh, Linda, but I'm telling you that there are a lot of changes coming to this household, and although your mother figures largely in them you're not entirely out in the cold. I thought you were going out! He hasn't got tired of waiting for you, has he?'

'I just want to have a few words with you, Lucy.' Linda sat down at the table and leaned forward, her voice dropping into undertones. 'Mother is coming in here shortly to have a word with you, and it's to do with what she's got on her mind. She has made a decision, and she thinks it is the right one. I want her to find that out for herself, so if she does confide in you please don't voice an opinion. Listen to her, and talk to her if you like, but don't say anything that might put her off.'

'You can trust me, Linda,' Lucy said slowly. 'I think the world of your mother. She's been a very good friend to me over the years, and anything I can do to help her will be done, don't you worry. Now you run along and take care of your own life. I don't for one moment think your mother needs any help to handle hers, but she'll find me full of common sense if she does confide in me.'

Linda squeezed the housekeeper's arm and got up to leave. 'I hope the changes won't be too great, Lucy,' she said in parting. 'But this could affect the whole household, not just Mother and me.'

Martin gave a great sigh of relief when Linda appeared in the sitting-room doorway, and came out of the room in a hurry, taking her arm as they walked along the hall. Linda half turned towards him and he bent quickly and kissed her cheek.

They left the house and Linda seemed to be walking on air. So this was love! It had really happened to her! She gripped his arm and held it as if she would never let him go, and they walked through the bright evening sunshine without a care in the world.

'This time last week,' he said, 'I was beginning to think of packing my things, and I was wondering what kind of a life I would find here. I never dreamed that there would be a girl waiting, and a girl who fits so many of the details I require in a woman.' His hand upon her arm tightened. 'Linda, I feel quite strongly about you. It might be too early to tell you, but I don't care. None of the customary ways of courting a girl seem to apply in our case, or perhaps they do and I don't know that I'm supposed to feel the way I do. It's love at first sight between us, you know that, don't you?'

'It's love for the first time in my life,' she replied. 'I have no experience to fall back on as a gauge. All I know is that you have suddenly become very important to me, and I should hate to lose you. Life before I met you was full enough, but it consisted of all work and no play. You've brought another dimension with you, Martin.'

'And that's exactly how I feel about you.' He put an arm around her waist and squeezed her affectionately. 'I wish a few months would quickly roll by. Then I would know a great deal more about you, and it wouldn't appear presumptuous if I started thinking about our future together.'

She glanced at him, and there was a keen expression in her eyes. He nodded slowly.

'I'm sorry if I'm going too fast for you,' he said. 'But that's how I feel about you.'

'We do have plenty of time,' she replied, 'but don't let time stand between us. We're not adolescents, and we should know our own minds by now.'

He held her tightly as they walked along the pavement, and Linda felt that the whole meaning of life had changed. Nothing seemed real any more. It was exactly as if she had donned rose-tinted spectacles. She had heard the expression used in love, and could not imagine anyone getting that way about anything. Now she knew differently, and it was all like some great dream come true.

They walked a long way, both reluctant to call the evening over, but darkness came and they had to turn back. There was peace inside Linda as they walked hand in hand, and she felt a warmth and security with Martin that she had never known before.

At ten-thirty they were almost home, and a car pulled into the kerb beside them and Robert stuck his head through the window.

'Hello,' he called. 'I thought I recognised you, Linda. Can I give you both a lift?'

'No, thanks,' Linda replied quickly. 'We're enjoying the walk.'

'Thanks for the offer,' Martin said.

'All right, I'll see you later.' Robert seemed reluctant to go on. 'Any change at home, Linda?' he queried.

'I've been out all evening, Robert. You'd better get on home and find out.'

He stared at her, trying to read something from her expression, but Linda smiled, and he nodded slowly and drove away. When his rear lights had vanished from sight Linda spoke slowly.

'He's asked Mother to marry him,' she said. 'That's what she's been in a flutter about all week-end, and this evening before we came out she had practically decided to accept him.'

'I see.' Martin nodded. 'Well, that will be a surprise for a lot of people. Robert must think a great deal of your mother. People I know are convinced that he would never marry again.'

'I know he was divorced, and I suppose a bad start like that is apt to put one against marriage completely, but he's very keen on Mother.'

'She's a very pleasant woman,' he said. 'Just my idea of a mother-in-law.'

Linda clung to his arm and they went on through the shadows. By the time they got home perhaps Robert would have learned his fate, and she hoped it would be a happy one.

When they arrived at the house it was obvious that Robert had been given a decision, and it was the right one, for a bottle of champagne stood on the small table in the sitting-room, and everyone was holding a filled glass. Stella and Colin were there, and Lucy and Mrs. Shelton, and they were obviously waiting for Linda and Martin to arrive.

Mrs. Shelton looked selfconscious, and her cheeks were stained with a girlish flush. Linda saw that her mother was happy, and she felt her heart start racing. At long last everything seemed to be working well.

Robert announced his engagement to Mrs. Shelton, and he produced a glittering diamond ring, which fitted Mrs. Shelton's finger perfectly. Everyone drank a toast to the happy couple, and the sitting-room echoed to the good wishes that were offered. Robert said a few appropriate words in his usual booming voice, and Linda went to her mother's side and hugged her.

'I'm sure I'm doing the right thing,

dear,' Mrs. Shelton said in an undertone. 'Robert is such a good, understanding man. But there are so many things which I must talk over with him. I think we'll be able to agree over some of the details.'

'Of course you will, Mother,' Linda told her. She glanced across the room and saw that Stella was behaving normally, holding Martin's attention, and poor Colin seemed rather forlorn sitting alone on the sofa, an empty champagne glass clutched in one hand.

They sat together for some time, talking generally, Martin between Linda and Stella, with Colin perched on the edge of the sofa on Stella's other side. Robert poured the last of the champagne into their glasses, and went back to Mrs. Shelton's side. Linda had never seen him so happy.

She studied her mother's face with critical gaze, and had to admit that she had never seen her mother so cheerful. Love could come at any age, she told herself, and glanced into Martin's eyes and felt happy at what she saw there.

Later that evening, when the others had gone to bed, Mrs. Shelton tapped at Linda's door and came into the room, wearing her red dressing-gown. Linda was at the dressing-table brushing her hair. Mrs. Shelton was nervous now, and she sat upon the foot of Linda's bed and watched her daughter for a moment.

'Do you think I'm doing the right thing, dear?' she asked at length.

Linda put down the brush and swivelled around in her seat. She regarded her mother with steady gaze. Then she smiled. 'So now you're having second thoughts,' she said. 'Well, that's to be expected. You're taking a big step and you want to be sure that it's right.'

She got up and crossed to the bed, sitting down beside her mother and taking her hands in a tight grip. 'I should go straight to bed and sleep soundly,' she advised. 'Right now your head is going round, isn't it?' Her mother nodded. 'Then do as I say, and I'm sure that in the morning everything will be in its right perspective.'

'Do you think so, dear? I'm so very happy, but there are nagging doubts, and I suppose that's to be expected. It is a big step, and I'm wondering if I'm equipped to deal with it.'

'Of course you are. Don't lose your confidence. You've got a good life before you if you face it squarely. Now you run along to bed and sleep well.'

'All right, dear. See you in the morning.' Mrs. Shelton kissed Linda and got slowly to her feet. She left the room, and Linda returned to brushing her hair. Happiness had come firmly to the house, she thought sleepily, and they would both make sure it stayed with them . . .

The next morning at breakfast Martin confessed that he felt like a new boy, and Stella demanded to ride in Linda's car with them. Gerald Olley winked at Linda as he prepared to leave.

'Come on, Stella,' he said firmly. 'You're not playing gooseberry. Act your age and leave them alone.'

'What are you talking about?' the girl demanded. 'They're still strangers. Don't throw them together, Gerald.' She eyed them both keenly, then shrugged and went out of the room behind the grinning Olley.

Robert was looking pensive, and it struck Linda that he was hanging back. He wanted to talk to her mother, she thought, and smiled.

'Come along, Martin, perhaps we'd better be going,' she said. 'Philip, would you like to ride with us this morning? Robert is going to be late for once, I do believe.'

'Really?' Norris glanced at Robert, and nodded. 'All right, I can read the signs. But I don't want to intrude upon you two.'

'Think nothing of it,' Linda said with a smile, checking her handbag for the car keys.

'I shall be coming along directly,' Robert said. 'I must have a word with your mother before I leave, Linda.' He glanced towards the kitchen door, moved uncertainly towards it, then paused. 'But I don't want Lucy to overhear,' he added.

Linda went to the kitchen and called to her mother. As Mrs. Shelton appeared Linda called good-bye to Lucy.

'Off now, dear? Be very careful on the road, won't you?'

'Yes, I'll be careful. Good-bye, Mother. Robert is waiting to talk to you before he leaves.'

Martin opened the back door for her, and then he and Philip Norris followed her out to the garage. Philip got into the back of the car and Martin sat beside Linda. She drove steadily to the hospital, and when they arrived in the car-park Norris took his leave quickly.

'I'll walk in with you, Linda,' Martin said. 'I've got to see Roland Marlow before I start working, and he won't be in yet, so I've been told.'

'I'll show you where my office is,' Linda told him. 'There is an unoccupied one next door, so perhaps you'll get that.'

'And don't forget that we both have the same day off,' he said with a smile. 'I'm certainly glad I arranged it like that. Just think of the nice days that will be coming up this summer.'

'If they don't switch the days around,' Linda replied pessimistically. 'That always happens in the summer, with people going off on holiday.'

They entered the hospital and Linda led the way to her office. Martin glanced around approvingly when he saw it. He watched her take off her light coat and put on the white one she wore in the wards. He came towards her, taking her gently into his arms, and when he kissed her she held her breath in ecstasy.

'Your kisses do something to me,' she whispered.

'That's how it should be,' he replied. 'I think we're very lucky to have found each other. A lot of people go through their entire lives without meeting the person intended for them.'

'You must be right, judging by the divorce rate,' Linda said. 'Now one more kiss and you'd better go and see Roland Marlow. It wouldn't do to keep him waiting. I shall be ready at twelve-thirty to go to lunch, so if you can arrange your working times to coincide with mine I shall be able to drive you home and bring you back.'

'I couldn't ask for a nicer chauffeuse,' Martin said with a smile. He kissed her again, sighed regretfully, and moved to the door. 'This is where the dreams fade a little and reality takes hold, but I've still got you, Linda. That part of it won't disappear.'

'I'll always be around,' she replied.

The morning seemed to go faster than usual, and she knew it was because she was impatient to see Martin again, to learn how he had been making out and to find out if he liked the hospital.

Just before noon she managed to get back to her office, and while she was there the telephone rang. Answering it, she heard Robert's voice. He sounded angry.

'Is that you, Linda?' he demanded.

'Yes, Robert. What's the trouble?'

'I'd like to talk to you before you go home to lunch. Can you possibly come to my office within the next few minutes?'

'Is it that important?' she demanded, glancing at her watch. 'I want to get along to the lab before lunch, and it's late now.'

'Your mother is important, isn't she?'

'Of course. But what's wrong?'

'Not over the phone, my dear girl. It would be all over the hospital in an hour.'

'All right, I'll be along to see you in a few moments.' Linda hung up and sat for a moment staring blankly into space. What had happened to upset Robert? He was usually a placid man.

She sighed and picked up the phone again, calling the lab, and asked if the reports she wanted were ready. Someone told her they would be on her desk by the afternoon, and she had to be satisfied with that. Leaving the office, she called into a ward to see a patient, then made her way to Robert's office.

Robert called a loud invitation for her to enter, and motioned for her to sit down.

'What seems to be the trouble with Mother?' Linda demanded.

'You know I stayed to speak with her this morning when you all came out,' Robert said heavily. 'Well, I gave her some idea of what I expect when we're married. Naturally, I'm against her running the boarding house. As my wife she will have a certain standard to maintain. I do a lot of entertaining, and until my marriage I have to do it in hotels. But with a wife and a home I shall expect to use the house.'

'You told Mother this and she refused to give up the guests?' Linda demanded.

'Flatly. Wouldn't even listen to reason. I was being reasonable. Running a boarding house is all right for a widow, but as the wife of a respected doctor there is such a thing as position to be maintained. In any case I should need more privacy after marriage. It isn't the thing for a wife to have half a dozen adult lodgers around the house all day.'

'You mentioned this to me before,' Linda said slowly. 'I wonder that you didn't make your views clear before you proposed. What did Mother have to say?'

'I've told you. She refused to consider giving up the guest house, as she calls it. I didn't have time to reason further with her, and I asked you here because I hope you will be able to help.'

'Just how can I help?' Linda asked slowly.

'Try and persuade your mother that it would be better to relinquish that business of hers.' Robert was still seething with indignation. 'She must be made to see that it just won't do. There must be sacrifices on either side, of course, and I shall be giving up my freedom, so I think it only fair that your mother should give in to my desire. It's hardly the thing for a marriage to start with a house filled with paying guests.'

'Are you sure you want to marry Mother?'

'What on earth do you mean?' Robert stared at her, silenced by the tone of her sharp voice.

'Just think it over carefully,' Linda said, turning to the door. 'I'll have a talk with Mother when I get home, but I shan't try to influence her in any way. It's something that you'll have to work out between yourselves, but don't try and drive Mother, Robert, because it won't work.'

'All right,' he said slowly. 'I'll try and have patience.'

6

Martin was waiting by the car when Linda arrived there, and he smiled happily when he saw her. She tried to drag her mind away from her thoughts, and her face was showing a troubled expression as she greeted him.

'Hello, Martin. What sort of a morning did you have?'

'Quite good, considering. I'm moving into that empty office next to you. But what's been happening to you? You look as if you've had a trying morning.'

'It's nothing to do with work,' she replied, getting into the car. She unlocked the door his side and he got in beside her. As she drove homewards she explained the talk she had just had with Robert, and when she lapsed into silence Martin shook his head.

'I shouldn't get involved in it, Linda,' he said seriously. 'As you told Robert, it's something they'll have to work out for themselves. They will find it difficult to settle down together, obviously, because they aren't young people. They're set in their habits, and neither of them will feel like giving way to the other. It will only work if they do have real feelings for one another.'

'That's exactly what I feel about it,' Linda said. 'But I do feel that Robert is being a bit high-handed. That is his way, of course, and he doesn't realise it. I told him not to drive Mother, and if he takes that advice then they might be able to work it out.'

'I don't think it is an unreasonable demand that Robert is making,' Martin said.

'No. I shouldn't want to start married life under those circumstances,' Linda agreed.

When they arrived at the house Gerald Olley's motorcycle was already parked outside. They entered, and Martin went into the sitting-room while Linda went through to the kitchen to find her mother.

Lucy was busy in the kitchen, but there was no sign of Mrs. Shelton, and the housekeeper was looking angry and flustered as she looked up at Linda.

'Thank heavens you're home, Linda!'

'What's wrong? Where's Mother?'

'She's packed a bag and gone,' Lucy said, shaking her head. 'I tried to get her to wait for you to return, but she was like a woman demented. She's gone.'

'Gone where?' Linda stared at the woman, unable to believe her ears. 'Why didn't you ring me, Lucy?'

'Because I didn't want to worry you. I thought she'd only be gone a few moments, but she hasn't come back. Who knows what was in her mind?'

'Have you managed all right alone?' Linda asked.

'Yes, everything is ready. Perhaps you'll help to serve. Don't worry, Linda. It's just nerves and fear. She won't come to any harm. She had a few high words with Robert this morning after you all left.'

'Yes, I know all about that. I spoke to

Robert just before I left the hospital. But I didn't think it would upset Mother so. Did she say where she might be going?'

'No. Just told me she wanted to get away from everyone for a few days. Said she would ring when she felt better. I thought it best to let her go without a lot of argument. She had a shock with that proposal coming out of the blue, and I'd say she's been living on her nerves for the past few days, although I'm no doctor.'

'Poor Mother!' Linda tied an apron around her waist and then washed her hands at the sink. She began to help Lucy with the meal, and opened the service hatch. Lucy started placing the plates on the counter, and Linda went out to the hall, calling that lunch was ready as she went into the dining-room. She began putting the plates on the table, and Martin came through with Stella at his side, then they were followed by Gerald Olley and Colin Lambert. Just as they were sitting down to the meal the front door slammed and Robert and Philip Norris appeared.

'I'd like to talk to you for a moment, Robert,' Linda said, moving to the door, and he stepped aside for her, then followed her into the sitting-room. He closed the door as she turned to face him, and his face tensed when he heard about Mrs. Shelton's departure.

'Good heavens!' he said. 'I had no idea she was so serious about this place.'

'It's been her whole life for a number of years,' Linda told him.

'But what can we do?' he demanded. 'We must find her. Have you no idea where she might have gone?'

'None at all. We have no close relatives around here.'

'What about that aunt in Scotland?' he asked, his face showing grave concern.

'Well, she won't reach there until some time tomorrow morning, so I shan't bother ringing today.'

'But aren't you worried about her, Linda?'

'Of course I am, but Mother is well

able to look after herself, and she said she wanted a few days on her own. She'll either ring or come back when she feels she can face us. She has gone through an ordeal this past week-end. Let her find her feet.'

'I'm inclined to ring the police and report her missing,' Robert said worriedly.

'No.' Linda's voice was firm. 'She's not missing in that sense. And she won't be away too long.'

'If you think so,' he agreed unwillingly. 'But I had no idea she would get so upset. I'm heartily sorry for this, Linda. When she does return I'll tell her that I'm sorry.'

'Your lunch will be getting cold,' Linda said. 'I shan't tell the others the truth about her going. If they ask I'll say that she needed a few days away from everything. They'll understand that.'

'Good girl!' Robert patted her shoulder, then turned to the door. 'I knew I could rely upon you to prevail with common sense.'

'Just treat her gently when she does return, Robert,' Linda said.

'I will,' he promised. 'I've still got a lot to learn, haven't I?'

Linda smiled and followed him into the dining-room, and when they were seated at the table she glanced around at the others.

'Mother went away this morning,' she said. 'She'll be gone for a few days.'

They accepted the news without much comment, and Linda was relieved. After the meal was over, she helped Lucy clear away, and in the kitchen, while the others were in the sitting-room, she broached the subject of running the house in her mother's absence.

'I'll get my sister to help, if you don't mind,' Lucy said. 'I can't run things alone.'

'Can you contact her this afternoon?' Linda asked, and Lucy nodded.

'She'll be here before you get back to tea,' the housekeeper said.

When it was time to return to the hospital Linda gave a great sigh of relief. She called into the kitchen on her way out to the car.

'You will call me if Mother gets in touch with you this afternoon, Lucy?'

'Of course, love. Don't you worry though.'

'Perhaps this is the best thing she could have done.' Linda paused to think about it. 'It's probably helped Robert get himself into perspective.'

'I said in the first place that she would be doing wrong if she tied herself to him,' Lucy said with a sniff. 'There's no sense in making a rod for your own back.'

'Robert isn't as bad as that.' Linda turned away. 'See you when I get back,' she called, and went out to the car.

'Is there some sort of a crisis in the house?' Martin asked as she drove towards the hospital.

'There is, but I'm hoping it will solve itself after a few days.' She explained how her mother had gone off. 'Do you think I'm doing the right thing by ignoring it?'

'I should think so. She is old enough to know what she's doing.'

Linda felt comforted by his words. 'I half expect Mother to be back home when we return this evening,' she said. 'If she isn't, I'll wait until morning, then ring Aunt in Scotland. It's about the only place she'll go.'

Soon Linda was driving into the hospital car-park. They left the car and walked towards the large building. When they reached the door of her office they parted. Linda went into her little room, and sighed as she sat down to start work. The reports she had asked for were on the desk, and she went through them carefully, pushing all personal thoughts into the background.

By the time the afternoon had passed Linda had brought herself up to date with her work. She returned to her office, and was tempted to put through a call to Lucy, but fought the impulse. Lucy had promised to ring if there was news, and there was no sense in making a nuisance of herself. Poor Lucy would be worried enough as it was.

Robert called, asking if there was any news, and she reported negatively. He sounded extremely worried, and she tried to console him. He hung up and she relaxed in her seat, and the silence that descended seemed to hang heavily. Where had her mother gone that morning? Why hadn't she rung the hospital to talk to her daughter?

Linda wished now she had given more time and thought to her mother's problems, but she had been too afraid that what she said might sway her mother into the wrong decision. But her mother had counted upon her for help, and she had failed her.

Linda was glad that it was almost time to go home. She felt terrible about the whole situation. When there was a tap at the door she started nervously, and hesitated before calling an invitation. The door opened and Martin came in. He closed the door and leaned against it.

'I've finished for the day,' he said.

'What about you?'

'I'm through,' she told him mechanically.

'You're looking worried, Linda. No word about your mother yet?'

'Nothing. I do hope she's all right.'

'Well, of course she'll be all right,' he said, coming around the desk and lifting her gently but firmly to her feet. 'What are you thinking about? You don't think she's gone off to do something silly, do you?'

'No, of course not.'

'I know it's very difficult for you to stop worrying, Linda, but that's what you've got to do. Your mother struck me as being a very capable woman, and I'm sure she knows what she's doing.'

He tilted her chin with a gentle hand and kissed her lightly on the lips. Linda slipped into his arms, pressing her face into his strong shoulder.

'I'm so glad you're here, Martin,' she said softly. 'I don't know what I'd do without you.'

'I'm glad to hear you say that,' he

told her seriously. 'I feel the happiest man in the world. Come on, let's get out of here for the day. There may be some word of your mother at home.'

Linda nodded, although she knew Lucy would have telephoned had her mother returned.

They went home, and the house seemed empty as they entered. Even without being told, Linda knew there was no news about her mother, but she hurried into the kitchen to see Lucy.

The housekeeper was doing the tea, and her eyes were red rimmed, as if she had been crying. For a moment Linda stared at the woman, wondering if there had been news of a kind, and she hardly dared to put her thoughts into words.

'Nothing to report,' Lucy said briskly, and it was obvious that she was trying to cover her emotions. 'In the morning you'd better ring Scotland.'

'I expect I shall have to,' Linda replied.

'Will you give me a hand with the tea?' Lucy continued. 'My sister won't be able to get here until tomorrow.'

Linda nodded. 'I'll just go up and change,' she said. 'Shan't be a moment.'

Her face hardened as she passed the door of the sitting-room and glanced in to see Stella perched on the arm of the big easy chair occupied by Martin, who was trying to read the newspaper. She hesitated, but did not go into the room. She ascended the stairs two at a time, and slammed the door of her room after she had entered.

There she paused and took a deep breath. She laughed suddenly, and the tension seemed to leave her. It was ridiculous getting her so jealous over Stella. She knew what Stella was like, and she knew that Martin wouldn't give the girl a second glance.

Changing her dress, Linda went down to the kitchen again to help with the tea. Robert came in at the front door as she reached the hall, and she shook her head in reply to his anxious query. His face seemed to drop as he nodded slowly. It was a fine start to their engagement, Linda thought, hurrying into the kitchen, and she threw herself into the work of helping with the meal in order to lose herself from her thoughts.

After the meal Linda helped with the washing-up, and Martin followed her into the kitchen to do the drying. He smiled at her when he caught her eye, and she nodded, trying to dispel the gloom that had slowly descended upon her since their arrival home. She was wondering about her mother. Where was she now? Why had she gone off without a word?

As they left the kitchen the front doorbell rang, and Linda excused herself and hurried to answer it, her heart in her mouth.

She pulled open the door, and then froze in horror. A policeman stood there, his face grim. Linda gasped, and her hand went to her mouth.

'Oh, no!' she gasped. 'Don't tell me something has happened to Mother!'

'This is the Shelton residence?' the

policeman asked.

'Yes. I'm Linda Shelton.'

'Does Mrs. Mavis Shelton live here?' He was inexorable in the execution of his duty.

'Yes.' Linda was almost frantic. 'Have you news of her?'

'She's in hospital at Brentchester, but there's no need to get alarmed. She's been injured, but she's in no danger.'

'What happened? How did she get to Brentchester?' Linda's wits were scattered in shock. 'Please, won't you come in off the step?'

'Thanks.' He removed his helmet as he stepped over the threshold. 'Don't worry too much,' he said consolingly. 'She was on a train that was derailed. No one was killed, but several passengers were injured, and she was one of them. I don't know the extent of her injuries, but they would have told us had they been really serious. Are you her next of kin?'

'Yes. Which hospital is she in, please?'

'The General Hospital, Brentchester.

I should ring them, if I were you. They'll soon put you right. Was she going on holiday, then?'

'For a few days,' Linda replied automatically.

'Well, I hope you'll find her in good shape. Good evening, miss. I'm sorry about the shock.'

'Thank you very much,' Linda responded, opening the door for him. He stepped outside, nodding respectfully before leaving, and she stood for a moment watching his departing figure.

'What did he want?' It was Robert at her back, and he grasped her shoulder and spun her around as she closed the door. 'It wasn't something to do with your mother, was it?'

Linda looked up into his pale face, nodding slowly, and she gave him the details as she had got them. Shock came into his brown eyes, and his face drained of blood.

'Oh, heavens!' he cried. 'This is all my fault. Brentchester General, you said?'

Linda nodded, incapable of speech now. She watched Robert hurry to the telephone on the small table, and she felt stifled as she listened to him getting the number of the hospital. Eventually he got through, and then his clipped tones demanded information. There was a delay, then he spoke briefly before listening intently. When he hung up the receiver his face was still ashen. He turned to face Linda.

'She's fractured her left leg and there are some broken ribs,' he said gravely. 'It's too early yet for them to know the full extent of her injuries. We can ring again in the morning.'

Linda closed her eyes and took a blind step towards him. He hurried to her side, holding her with his strong, gentle hands, and she heard him calling for Martin. The next moment Martin was at her side, holding her, demanding to be told what had happened. She listened in a daze as Robert's voice told of the accident and her mother's injuries, but she couldn't believe it. It just couldn't be true!

'Come and sit down, Linda,' Martin said, leading her into the sitting-room. He helped her on to the sofa and joined her, holding her comfortingly.

Robert fetched some brandy, and Linda almost choked on it, but she felt better after she had swallowed some.

'I must go to her,' she said at once.

'You're in no fit state to drive up there,' Martin said. 'It's all of a hundred and sixty miles. But perhaps you'll be going as well, Robert?'

'I have a right to go, but I don't know how they'll take it at the hospital,' Robert replied. 'One of us off because of an emergency is bad enough, but two of us!'

'You could drive up now, and probably get back early tomorrow morning. It will be a bit of a push, but someone should go with Linda.' Martin spoke reluctantly. 'I should like to go with her, but you do have the right, Robert, and most probably it would do Mrs. Shelton more good to see you there at her bedside.'

'Of course.' Robert nodded emphatically. 'All this is my fault. If I hadn't been so darned stupid this morning none of it would have happened. She would have stayed right here with us.' There was agony in his tones, and Linda smiled gently as she looked up at him.

'Don't blame yourself, Robert. It wasn't your fault. It's just one of those things. Will you drive up with me? I'm sure she'll be glad to see the both of us.'

'Yes. I must do everything I can to reassure her. I don't care in future if she wants to run a string of hotels. Martin, perhaps you'll explain the situation at the hospital in the morning if I don't happen to be back in time. But I won't stay up there longer than to find out the general condition. If she's in no danger I'll come straight back.'

'I don't know what clothes she took with her,' Linda said, getting to her feet. 'But knowing Mother, she will have taken along everything she needs for a trip.'

'We'll go in my car,' Robert said. He glanced at his watch. 'We should be there before midnight. I'll just get a small case, in the event that we do stay over there, and I suggest you do the same, Linda.'

She nodded and left the room, and Martin went with her, following her into her room, and he sat on the foot of her bed while she put a few essentials into a small case. When she was ready to leave he got up and stood in front of her.

'I hope you'll find her in a comfortable condition, Linda,' he said gently, and she threw the case upon the bed and hurled herself into his arms. She began to cry, and he patted her shoulder consolingly. 'I wish I was going along with you,' he went on, 'but you'll be all right with Robert. Stay up there if you wish, and I'll explain it at the hospital. You'll ring me here or at the hospital, won't you?'

'Yes,' she whispered, feeling for a handkerchief. 'I'm so glad you're here,

Martin. I don't know what I'd do without you.'

He kissed her gently, and then took her case, leading her out of the room and down the stairs. Robert was waiting in the hall, and he opened the front door for her. Martin went outside with them, and as they drove away he stood waving from the gate, and Lucy stood on the doorstep, waving pathetically, her face showing the same shock that gripped both Linda and Robert.

For a long while they were both silent in the car. Time passed as if it didn't exist, and darkness came. Robert switched on the lights, and still the car raced on.

'It's all my fault,' Robert said in agonised tones. 'What a fool I am! I should have known just how sensitive your mother is. I shall never forgive myself over this.'

Linda did not answer, and Robert remained silent after that, concentrating upon driving to Brentchester as fast as he could.

When they reached the hospital,

Robert parked the car and they got stiffly from it. Linda followed him numbly, her emotions frozen now. She felt herself in the grip of unreality.

Presently they reached an office, and she stood in the background while Robert made some enquiries. She could hear the mumble of voices, but failed to get any sense from them. When Robert came back to her she shook herself clear of the shock that had gripped her from the moment she had seen the policeman on the doorstep, and took a deep breath as she listened to what Robert had to say.

'She's had an emergency operation,' he told her, 'and her condition is satisfactory. Her life is in no danger, Linda.' There was relief in his voice and in his fleshy features. 'Thank goodness!' he said feelingly. 'Come along, she's in Grant Ward, and we can just peep in at her.'

Linda nodded dumbly, and followed him. A man in a white coat appeared in the doorway of the ward as they approached, and Robert greeted him like a long lost brother.

'Adams!' he cried. 'Are you still here, then? It's good to see you, old chap.'

'Robert Pearce! What on earth are you doing here?'

'Visiting Mrs. Shelton. She's one of the casualties from the local train derailment. This is her daughter, Dr. Linda Shelton. She's with me at St. Margaret's in Redford.'

'How do you do, Dr. Shelton. Your mother's condition is satisfactory. You have no cause for alarm. She's in no danger. Come this way and you can see her. She's still under at the moment. We didn't bring her back up until fifteen minutes ago.'

Linda followed them into the dimly-lit ward, and there were screens around her mother's bed. Adams held the curtain aside for them, and Linda stared at her mother's face as if she had never seen it before.

Mrs. Shelton was still unconscious. Her legs were in a cage under the bedclothes. She looked so small and defenceless that Linda had to suppress a sob. Robert instinctively felt the pulse of the thin white arm that lay out of the clothes, and he met Linda's eyes and nodded approvingly. They tiptoed out of the ward and paused in the corridor.

'I shall have to get back to Redford in the morning,' Robert said. 'Can you fix us both with sleeping accommodation for a few hours, Adams, old chap?'

'Certainly, Robert. Anything for you.'

'Dr. Shelton will be staying on here tomorrow. It will be morning before we find out exactly how her mother is. I want to stay until I can have a few words with her.'

'That will be all right,' Adams said. 'Come with me. I think we can fix you up for one night.'

They walked along the corridor behind him, and Robert took Linda's elbow.

'She's going to be all right, Linda,' he said firmly. 'I am so relieved, and I know you must be. It's been a terrible shock, and it shouldn't have happened.

I've been a fool, but I intend changing all that in the very near future.'

Linda did not answer. Relief was beginning to chase out the shock that gripped her.

Adams kept going along the interminable corridors, and then they waited while he went into an office to talk to a night sister. When he reappeared he was smiling.

'Robert, you can have the use of my room for the night, and Sister has sent for a nurse to take Dr. Shelton across to the nurses' home. That's the best I can do for you. I shall be on duty all night, Dr. Shelton, and I shall be keeping a close eye on your mother. I think you'll find her satisfactory in the morning.'

'Thank you so much,' she said.

'Anything to help,' he replied. 'Will you wait here while I take Robert away? You'll be able to meet at Grant Ward in the morning.'

Linda nodded, and Robert patted her shoulder.

'Try and get a good night's sleep,

Linda,' he said. 'I'll see you in the morning before I start back. Good night.'

'Good night, Robert,' she said wearily, and watched him go off along the corridor. Moments later a nurse appeared and led her away. When she was shown into a small room in the nurses' home she sank upon the bed and closed her eyes. It took a great effort for her to undress and prepare for sleep, and when she finally got into the bed she lay for a moment in the darkness, filled with the strangeness of it all, and then she drifted into sleep and knew nothing more until the early morning . . .

When she awoke Linda lay for a moment staring around the room, wondering where she was, and then it all came back to her and she sat up swiftly, horror flooding her mind. She took a deep breath and sprang out of bed, dressing quickly and hurrying along the corridor to find the wash-room.

Every fear she had ever known returned to her mind, and she wasted no time in getting across to the hospital. When she reached Grant Ward she found Robert in the Sister's office. He looked thoroughly at home.

'Hello, Linda,' he greeted. 'Don't look so worried. Your mother is comfortable this morning. I haven't seen her yet. They'll let us go along in a moment. Then I suggest we go and have breakfast somewhere. We can come back in an hour and talk to your mother, then I'll have to go back to Redford. But you stay on here as long as you like. I'll explain everything at the other end.'

Adams appeared in the doorway and beckoned them to follow him. They entered the ward, and Linda saw that her mother was still asleep. They stood for a few moments, just looking at her. Robert wouldn't even take her pulse for fear of disturbing her, and they departed silently. In the corridor Robert turned to her, his face bright and his dark eyes gleaming.

'Thank heavens she's going to be all right,' he said. 'She'll be up and about in about a month, Linda, and when we get her home we must take very good care of her. Adams, I want you to arrange for her to be placed in a private ward. Never mind the expense. I'll settle all that. Give her the best of everything, all the extras, you understand?'

'It will be done,' Adams replied.

'Good. Come along, Linda, and we'll get some breakfast. You must be hungry.'

'If you come back here about nine you'll be able to talk to her for a few moments,' Adams said.

Linda thanked him, and went with Robert. They left the hospital, found a café and had a good breakfast. She felt better afterwards, and animation began flowing through her. When it was time to return to the hospital they left the café and walked the short distance. They were permitted into the ward to see Mrs. Shelton.

Linda stared critically at her mother as they reached her bedside. Mrs. Shelton was conscious, and she smiled wanly at them. Linda walked to one side of the bed and Robert took the other. Mrs. Shelton glanced from one to the other of them, and tears sprang to her eyes.

'I am sorry for all this trouble I've caused you,' she said tremulously. 'I've been an utter fool!'

'No,' Robert said gently, 'I was the fool, but I can assure you, dear Mavis, that it will be different when we get you home.'

Linda bent over and kissed her mother, and Mrs. Shelton's arms came up around her neck.

'Linda, dear, I shouldn't have come away without first talking to you. I realise that now. If I had been killed it would have been on your mind for the rest of your life. Will you forgive me?'

'There's nothing to forgive,' Linda said. 'If anyone is to blame, then it's me. I should have seen that all the excitement and the shock would have been too much for you. I should have known better, Mother. But try and forget it now. It's all over. You won't have any worries when you come back home. You'll be able to do exactly as you please.'

'That's a fact,' Robert declared. 'You'll run the house as you please. I don't think I'd really want it any other way, come to think of it. When you're well enough to be moved I'm having you brought back to St. Margaret's, and then we'll soon have you back on your feet. You've got nothing to worry about now, so lie here and rest, and get well.'

'You're both very good to me,' Mrs. Shelton said wanly. 'How will they manage at the hospital without the both of you there?'

'I'm going back when we leave now,' Robert said. 'But Linda can stay on if she wants to. I can put that right when I get back.'

'No,' Mrs. Shelton said firmly. 'I want you both to go back to Redford. In a week they'll transfer me to your hospital, and you'll both be able to take care of me. But I should like to be left alone here to think things over quietly. I appreciate your concern, and I'm sorry you've had to rush over here. You must have worried terribly about me. But you both go back today.'

'If that's what you want, Mother,' Linda said. She smoothed Mrs. Shelton's hair back from her forehead. 'This is Tuesday. I have Friday off, and so does Martin. We'll come over for the day to see you.'

'And next week you'll be coming back to Redford,' Robert said. He leaned forward and took Mrs. Shelton's hand. 'Can you ever forgive me, my dear? I've been extremely short-sighted, haven't I?'

He bent forward and kissed her cheek, and tears rolled down her face. Linda held her mother's hand, and she felt like crying, but in relief. It seemed to her that the complications had fled. Her mother would be happy in the future. Robert would see to that.

They took their leave and went down to the car. It was a wonderful morning, and Robert was humming to himself as he drove out of the hospital.

'Stop when you see a telephone box, Robert, please,' Linda told him. 'I want to ring Martin. He'll be getting anxious now.'

'He's a lucky man,' Robert remarked. 'I wonder if I might make a prediction?'

'And what's that?' Linda prepared to slip out of the car as he brought it to a halt at the kerb opposite a telephone booth.

'That there is the likelihood of a double event taking place on the day I marry your mother,' he said with a smile.

'You know when you're on a good thing,' Linda told him. 'I wouldn't bet against that.'

She left the car and entered the telephone box, calling St. Margaret's hospital and asking for Dr. Crossley. A thrill tremored through her when she heard his voice in her ear.

'Martin,' she said. 'I just had to ring you. Mother's going to be all right.'

'I know,' he replied. 'I rang the hospital earlier. I'm so glad, Linda. I'm sure you must be very relieved.'

'My heart is jumping like a cat on hot bricks.' She laughed. 'I'm on my way home, Martin, and I can't wait to see you.'

'It's going to be a long morning,' he replied, 'but I shall be counting the minutes. Before you hang up, there's something I must tell you. It's about Stella. She made my life a misery last evening after you and Robert left. I did the only thing I could think of to really put her off.'

'And what was that?'

'I told her that I was in love with you, and would probably end up marrying you.' He laughed joyously, and she thrilled to the sound of it. 'I know it was a diabolical liberty,' he went on, 'but it has been effective. Stella won't talk to me now.' He paused, but Linda made no reply. 'You're not angry about that, are you?' he asked.

'Certainly not, you foolish man!' Linda laughed. 'But in all probability I shall hold you to your word. I hope there were witnesses present when you made that statement.'

'What kind of a fool do you think I am?' he teased. 'Of course there were witnesses. I made sure of that, and I hope you will hold me to it. Now hurry back here, will you?'

'I'm on the way, but my heart is already there,' she whispered as she hung up.

We do hope that you have enjoyed reading this large print book.

Did you know that all of our titles are available for purchase?

We publish a wide range of high quality large print books including:
Romances, Mysteries, Classics
General Fiction
Non Fiction and Westerns

Special interest titles available in large print are:
The Little Oxford Dictionary
Music Book, Song Book
Hymn Book, Service Book

Also available from us courtesy of Oxford University Press:
Young Readers' Dictionary
(large print edition)
Young Readers' Thesaurus
(large print edition)

For further information or a free brochure, please contact us at:
Ulverscroft Large Print Books Ltd.,
The Green, Bradgate Road, Anstey,
Leicester, LE7 7FU, England.
Tel: (00 44) 0116 236 4325
Fax: (00 44) 0116 234 0205

A HEART'S WAGER

Heidi Sullivan

Eva Copperfield has lived a life of poverty in the squalid slums of New York — until a sudden inheritance gives her the chance of a new life as lady of the manor in the English countryside. Her journey from rags to riches is complicated by the mysterious Ben — who is either a lord or a charlatan! Eva has to navigate the Atlantic and her heart before she can find a home . . . and love. Wagers are being made. Who will win?